KU-444-189

'I know you're not an editor,' Bennet said. 'I'm giving you a chance to be one.' He caught the look of disbelief, the slight curl of the upper lip. 'I'm not doing you a favour. I'm just recognising what other people are too stupid to see. Including yourself. You think you've done very well, but your talent has been wasted, buried in the middle of the bloody desert.'

Paula looked away from him to the pool table, and saw the Lebanese desert again and Ian smiling at her.

'I'll give you the *Register*,' he continued, '– a free hand. You'll be a double outsider – a woman and a reporter. That will shake up the bastards.'

Jack Ramsay

## *Inside Story*

based on a television series by
Peter Ransley

Sphere Books Limited

First published in Great Britain by Sphere Books Ltd
27 Wrights Lane, London W8 5TZ
Novelisation copyright © Sphere Books Ltd 1986
Based on an original concept by Anglia T.V. Limited
and Peter Ransley. © Peter Ransley 1986

TRADE
MARK

This book is sold subject to the condition that it shall not,
by way of trade or otherwise, be lent, re-sold, hired out or
otherwise circulated without the publisher's prior consent
in any form of binding or cover other than that in which it is published
and without a similar condition including this condition
being imposed on the subsequent purchaser.

Set in Linotron Ehrhardt

Printed and bound in Great Britain by
Cox & Wyman Ltd, Reading

# Part One

# One

*ex croxley*
*pro foreign: attn macdonald*
*standfirst*
*tank – one*
*for forty-eight hours last week, the armed forces of israel and syria faced one another on red alert, and a full-scale war appeared imminent following an attack on an israeli border post by a breakaway muslim group.*
*using three tanks painted with syrian markings, members of the fanatical shi'ite islamic jihad (holy war) attacked from the south lebanese side of the border in the early hours of thursday morning, destroying the post and killing three soldiers. within hours, israeli tanks crossed into the disputed territorial area north of bariyas where they encountered legitimate syrian tanks. i watched the battle and saw three tanks, two syrian and one israeli, knocked out. the battle lasted for an hour. the israeli air force was on red alert. a new middle east war seemed inevitable. full story upcoming.*

A grunt from the driver made the woman look up. Ahead, through the windshield of the jeep, she saw a cluster of whitewashed buildings shimmering in the heat haze. The jeep slowed and bumped over rutted tracks. She put her notebook in her pocket, then squinted ahead once more. One of the buildings carried a Coca-Cola sign. The driver glanced at her. She checked her watch and nodded. A moment later, the jeep shuddered to a halt. She reached for her camera, slung it round her neck and got out, the driver following her to the shade of the buildings.

There was no one around. It was the hottest time of the day. Only mad dogs and Englishwomen, she thought . . . and not even a mad dog in sight.

The driver had found some shade, slithered into a crouch and closed his eyes. She shivered in the heat, clutched her arms around her chest and walked across the dust road to the café. For three days, the sun had blasted into her and scrambled her brains and made her shiver, but she could cope with the heatstroke. It was the fear that was the problem. The fear produced adrenalin and the adrenalin kept her awake and alert, but later there would be a price to pay and she knew that soon she would have to leave the Lebanon. She had had enough. The country was ageing her.

A child, half naked and half asleep, blocked the entrance to the café. She stepped over him and looked in. The place was empty except for a fat man in a soiled apron behind the counter. A fan stirred the hot air. As she went inside, she felt as if she were entering a bowl of soup. Pots steamed behind the counter. She looked at them, ordered a plate of fish and a beer and glanced again at her watch. There was time. Soon she would be able to relax. Beirut was an hour away. She would finish scribbling the story in the jeep, type it out in her hotel room and, with luck, phone it through to London. If she could not get through, she would have it telexed. Once the acknowledgement came back from the office, she could relax; but not totally – not until she was sure she had made the editions. Then she would relax with a vengeance.

Then the man behind the counter was shouting something at her, some kind of warning and, as she dived to the floor, she heard the roar of a car engine coming from the east, followed by the first shots rattling the shutters. The sound of Armalites, she reckoned, calculating, trying, even in that moment of terror, to identify the gunmen. She heard the child cry and she looked over her shoulder. He had crawled inside, thumb in his mouth. Two figures carrying guns ran past the

4

window and the sound of the car receded into the west.

She waited until there was silence, then she got to her feet and padded to the door. The child was unhurt. She looked out. Her driver had vanished. The jeep bled oil and water into the dust. Slowly the children began to emerge from darkened doorways, silent at first then laughing and chattering, little coughing Arabic sounds, looking first at the jeep, then at her. The tallest came forward, a tattered urchin with narrowed eyes. He looked her up and down, taking in the dirty safari suit and the cropped red hair, his gaze lingering on her hair. He had probably never seen red hair, she thought, and he was making a simple calculation. A stranger with a camera. Two and two added up and meant money.

'Beirut?' he asked.

She nodded.

'I know a man with a car.' His voice was an American drawl.

She produced a note and he sneered at it. 'It is a very good car,' he added.

Another note, accompanied by a flash of her hands, indicated take it or leave it. He took it and beamed. She dragged her rucksack from the jeep and followed him, glancing again at her watch. Less than two minutes had passed.

Ten minutes later she was heading north again, in an old sedan. The driver was a small man with a big paunch, probably, she thought, the boy's father. They had agreed a price and he drove fast, one hand on the wheel, the other picking up nuts from the dashboard. A crucifix swung from the roof at eye level.

'American?' he asked.

'British,' she said. 'Sorry. No dollars.'

He shrugged. 'So, still I will have to save for my suitcase.'

She looked at him, puzzled.

'Every time the Israelis come back,' he continued, 'people say you must leave Beirut with a suitcase or in a coffin.' He grinned at her. 'I am still here.'

She smiled at him and looked at her watch again. London was two hours behind. They would be coming out of morning conference by now. The Editor would have asked where she was. They would know that the Israelis had come back. The Syrians had said so. Tel Aviv had denied it. They would know all this and would be waiting for her to check in. Bill Macdonald, the Foreign Editor, would have been given an uncomfortable couple of minutes. The Editor would want to know why she hadn't been in contact for three days and Bill would have had to stall.

Soon they would be dispersing for lunch. David Clare, the Editor, would be heading for one of his favourite restaurants. Toby Greene, his deputy, would stay behind with a sandwich, looking after the shop. Alan Merton, the News Editor, and Bill Macdonald would probably be in the back bar of the Harrow having a couple of lagers and it would be a gentle lunch for all of them. They could not afford to relax yet. Idly, she wondered what they had planned for the front and what chance she had of making the splash; a good chance, she thought, so long as nothing else big happened.

The outskirts of Beirut lay ahead. Smoke hung as an unnatural cloud above the city. In her mind she thought she could hear gunfire, but it was probably just the hum of distant traffic. The trouble was that everything sounded like gunfire to her these days.

The road had narrowed, sand-banks rising five or six feet on either side. Ahead she saw a sharp right-hand bend. Once round that, they would have a clear run towards the city. She knew where she was now. She had travelled this route before. The driver was singing softly as he eased the car round the bend, then he cursed and hit the brakes hard. The woman, her mind still in London, was thrown forward, her head smacking against the windscreen. She blinked, rubbed her forehead and saw a lorry, twenty yards away, blocking the road. It was broadside on to them, the windows smashed; a rifle aimed at them through shattered glass.

The driver reached for the crucifix and stroked the body of

Christ, watching and listening. There was a shout and a young man appeared from the back of the lorry and ran towards them. He was thin, with a dark fuzz of a beard and carried a rifle. Again the driver cursed. This was no Christian. He wrenched the crucifix free, tucked it under the mat at his feet, then reached into the glove compartment, pulled out a battered copy of the Koran and murmured, 'There is only one God and Allah is his prophet.'

The woman glanced at him, then pulled out her notebook, ripped the scrawled page out and crumpled it onto the floor. Ahead, the youth ducked behind a rock pile and began yelling at them, first in Arabic, then in French, to get out of the car. It was her turn to curse now. She'd been through many roadblocks. Sometimes it only took a minute, sometimes longer, but she didn't need this, not now. She had a fucking deadline for Christ's sake!

The driver looked to his left, at a dust road leading west at right angles. The youth was still yelling at them, brandishing his rifle. The driver watched him for a moment, then pushed his door open. The woman took her cue from him and got out, hauling out her rucksack and camera. Slowly she walked towards the lorry, then stopped as she realised the driver was not behind her. She turned as she heard the roar of the engine and saw the car backing away up the side road, the wheels squealing, throwing up a dust-storm around her, pricking her with grit, the driver unseen, low in the seat, only his hands visible on the wheel, strangling it as he hit the throttle. Then shots were fired, and again she was diving for cover. She lay motionless for a moment, then looked up to see the youth firing at the car, a second youth coming from the lorry towards her. Slowly she got to her feet.

The sedan was a hundred yards away now, moving fast and, as she watched, the driver sat up and held up a hand through the window, a fluttering wave of goodbye, then, ahead of him, figures moved into the road; more rifles, directly ahead. She closed her eyes but she could not help hearing the man die. When she opened her eyes, the car had smashed into a wall.

7

Steam hissed from the bonnet, the driver's door swung on its hinges, and his arm hung limp. Then she was being dragged away, a rifle pressed into her back, the smell of unwashed bodies assailed her, and curses were coughed into her face. She was pushed against the lorry and forced to her knees.

She glared at them through her sunglasses, yelled at them the word they all knew: *sahafi* (journalist) but they did not respond, merely slouched against the lorry. She struggled to her feet and a rifle was aimed at her head. She sat again and waited. There was nothing else for it. If they did not react to *sahafi*, they would react to nothing. All she could do was wait and hope that someone would come along who knew which end was up.

A minute later a car appeared from the north and drew up beside the lorry. A young man got out, as slim as the others, not yet twenty she thought, wearing a gaudy T-shirt, jeans and sneakers. Anywhere else he might have been heading for a rock concert, but not in this country.

The others had straightened out of their lethargy, showing respect. This was some kind of leader. In her bag was her Press card, her photograph and her name: Paula Croxley, *Sunday Register*.

She scrabbled in her bag but a rough hand slapped her and she stopped. Then the young man lazily leant forward and drew the sunglasses from her face, tried them on, then flung them over his shoulder, looking at her as the others fought in the dirt for ownership of them.

'Look,' she said, 'let me prove who I . . .'

The young man shook his head, leant inside the corpse of the lorry, pulled out an oily rag, then suddenly and violently grabbed her hair and forced her head back. Her mouth opened in protest and he stuffed the rag between her teeth. She stumbled, dizzy, with the stench of oil clogging her senses, fighting for breath and only vaguely aware of being dragged towards the car and flung inside.

The journey took half an hour. Twice she thought she was going to faint. Three times she tried to pull the gag out but they were too quick for her. It was a battle just to breathe, but eventually the car stopped and she was bundled out. She looked around but did not recognise her surroundings – just a Beirut suburb, the walls scarred by bullets and shells. Someone grabbed her from behind. She felt a hand rough on her breast and she kicked back and connected, spun away and glared at them. The classic rule was never to show fear. They could smell fear and, like animals, they might attack – but what she was thinking was an insult to animals, for among animals, there was no such thing as rape . . .

Then she was being pushed through a door, along a corridor and into a darkened room. The youngest drew the rag from her mouth. It was the sweetest release she had known. Instinctively she gulped air and choked, then the door was slammed shut and she was alone . . .

For an hour she sat in a corner, knees drawn up to her chin, a trembling mass of fear, frustration and anger. Every few minutes she looked at her watch. Obscenities flowed from her like vomit. She felt her cheek and found blood. There was a bump on her head from when they had thrown her into the car. Consciously she fought her fear with anger, making use of the adrenalin, cursing them. Upstairs she could hear voices. They would be discussing her, what to do with her. She had tried battering on the door but there was no response, and so she swore, long and loud. She had a story and a half, but it was useless in her pocket and in a few hours it would be redundant. She looked up as she heard a clatter of footsteps coming down the stairs, then blinked as the door was pushed open. The young man and the youngest youth stood framed in the doorway for a moment, the leader holding her bag, the other her camera.

She got to her feet and folded her arms.

'Please phone the Algerian chargé d'affaires,' she said in a steady voice. 'He will vouch for me.'

'You are American,' the leader said.

'I am British,' she insisted.

He smiled, reached into her bag and held out a small green

card, ran his finger along the embossed name. It was absurd. She checked herself. She had almost laughed in his face.

'That's a credit card,' she said. 'Anyone knows . . .'

Then they were on her, dragging her to her feet. She struggled and got a back-handed slap across the nose, which brought tears of pain and anger. Kicking and elbowing, she pushed herself away from them and stood, her back against the wall, spitting defiance. Then she made her big gamble, took a chance. The taxi driver had given her a clue. If she was wrong, she was in trouble. 'I'm writing about the Islamic Jihad,' she said. The leader frowned and stepped back. 'I have interviewed Kamal Bizri.'

For a moment there was silence, both young men frowning, confused, then the leader stepped close so that they were face to face.

'Where?' he asked.

'In the Bequaa Valley.'

'Where in the Bequaa Valley?'

'I was blindfolded.'

He stepped back and sneered at her. 'You're lying.'

'I have photographs,' she said and moved away from him, pointing at the camera, the youth holding it up, playing with the viewfinder.

'Don't touch it,' she shouted. 'The film has to be developed. I promised Kamal Bizri I would publish the reason why the Islamic Jihad has sworn to kill every American in Lebanon.'

Another moment of silence. She had the advantage, saw the gap and went for it. 'I have stories of atrocities, killings by Israel's puppet army in the south. If they are not published, Kamal Bizri will be displeased.'

*Displeased*. She liked that. Displeased meant to these two that their balls were in danger.

The leader leant back against the wall and snapped his fingers. 'I can read some English,' he said. 'Show me your story.'

She held out her hand for her bag and he passed it over.

10

Her notebook nestled between packs of Marlboro. She took it out, flipped the cover over and held it out.

Gregg shorthand. It could almost have been Arabic. The young man looked at the scrawl and shook his head. Paula looked into her bag and reached for her Press card. It was useless. If they didn't know American Express from a passport, then a Press card was of less use than a bus pass.

She'd played her hand, used up her ace of trumps, now all she could do was wait and see if she had won.

# Two

Debbie Cartwright stepped out of the cab into Park Lane, skipped quickly through the revolving doors into the foyer of the Grosvenor House Hotel, smiled at the reception desk and acknowledged the admiring glances of three men on their way out. She felt good. A week's skiing in Verbiers had topped up her tan. A quiet supper last night with brother Charles and eight hours' sleep made her feel like a teenager. On the way to the lifts, she briefly checked her appearance in a mirror. She would do, she thought. In three years she would be thirty – but three years was a long time.

In the lift taking her to the floor of apartments, she wondered idly what this man Bennet would be like. All she knew about him was that he was English, but had made his money in America in newspapers and was looking for a PA. Charles had met a New Yorker called Schiff last night, a 'little Jewish chappie', who'd told him that his boss was looking for someone with class and connections. John Bennet, the little chappie had said, wasn't the kind to go to agencies.

She imagined that he would be rather coarse. All Press people were coarse, weren't they? Tough-minded and driven by ambition, all that sort of thing. Hardly the kind of man that Debbie was accustomed to, but, she had to admit, he did not waste time. Last night she had typed out a brief c.v., had it biked round to him this morning and now, just two hours later, she had been invited for a meeting.

Yes, this Bennet wasted no time. Plus, he had money. Anyone who could afford an apartment in the Grosvenor

12

House Hotel wasn't low-rent. The question was, did he have style?

The lift stopped. She went down a carpeted corridor, stopped at the third door, glanced at her face in her little hand mirror, and knocked.

'Come in.' A deep voice. 'The door's open.'

She pushed it and walked into a small reception room. Beyond, through an open door, she saw Bennet seated behind a desk. He got to his feet and smiled as she moved towards him. He was tall, six-three maybe, with dark curly hair. The suit was expensive and too shiny to be English. He was suntanned. His smile displayed expensive dentistry, and, briefly, she felt an unaccustomed tremor of nervousness. Debbie Cartwright hadn't felt nervous since she was at school. There was nothing and no one in her life to feel nervous about. Bennet gestured to a seat and she sat opposite him and looked around. His desk was a mass of papers, telexes and computer print-outs. The far wall was dominated by a film poster in a frame:

ANN VAN LEIGH
in
SUMMER

The face of the actress smiled down at her. Debbie vaguely remembered hearing about the film, but she hadn't seen it. Seven, eight years ago she was into Truffaut and Rafelson; wouldn't have been seen dead watching some Kleenex movie.

To her right the telex gurgled into life. She glanced at the word processor and the print-out machine and swore a silent oath. She'd never been near one of those things and maybe this would be a problem.

Bennet was being polite now, asking how she was, thanking her for coming so quickly and offering a drink. She refused, her mind working automatically, trying to pigeon-hole him by his accent. It was what was called 'mid-Atlantic' – classless and hard to categorise.

No, she said, she didn't want a drink. She saw her c.v.

13

nestling among the telexes, saw Bennet glance at it then up at her.

'As my personal secretary and assistant, Miss Cartwright, you would play a key role in the running of my UK newspaper group.'

She looked again at the screen of the word processor. It was green and blank and seemed to her, at that moment, like some mechanical enemy.

'I haven't put word processing down on my c.v.,' she said, 'but . . .'

'Excellent,' he said.

Excellent? She blinked.

Then he glanced at her legs.

'Excellent,' he repeated.

Oh shit, she thought. Surely not? He wouldn't be so . . . Then he was picking up a copy of the *Tatler*, flipping through and handing it to her.

'Do you know any of these people?' he asked.

She took it and glanced at it. The society page. Young men in dinner jackets, women in frocks and pearls, the photographs numbered, the captions in a box on the left-hand page. There was Amanda with her mouth open as usual; and Simon leering at some anonymous cleavage.

'I went to school with her,' she said, pointing to Amanda, then to Simon. 'And he's a mate.'

'Excellent,' he said again. 'Any questions?'

She blinked. Nothing more from him? The ball in her court already? She searched for something intelligent to say.

'How many newspapers do you own here, exactly?'

'None, exactly,' he replied. 'Yet. But the road from Wapping is lined with opportunities.'

Debbie nodded. It was time to get down to basics.

'Salary?'

'Fifteen thousand,' he said.

She sat straighter.

'Is that acceptable?' he asked.

It was more than acceptable and she told him so. He smiled

14

at her and she realised then one of the reasons the man was a success. He had a smile that was a lyric from a pop song. It lit up the room. It could melt hearts of stone. It could bring knickers down. And he was holding out his hand. She took it. It was dry and firm.

'This is worth more than any contract,' he said. 'You can start now.'

He dropped her hand as she gaped at him.

'I know it's Saturday, Debbie, but I work at weekends, like Napoleon marched at night. It takes people by surprise.'

She looked at him enquiringly and he filled the silence with an answer.

'I'm lunching with Frank Ormsby, Managing Director of the *Sunday Register*.'

There was a notepad on his desk, virgin white. She flipped it open and wrote: lunch – Ormsby. When she looked up he was already at the door and she thought of her eight hours' sleep and reckoned that, from now on, eight hours would be a luxury.

The Bentley eased its way west through the Fleet Street traffic and Frank Ormsby stretched his legs and yawned, fighting to force the tension out of his body. He had a hangover. Last night Marjory had given him a surprise party for his fifty-fifth birthday and, to be truthful, he could have done without it. He was too tired. There had been too much on his mind lately and not enough hours in the day.

Unexpectedly he caught sight of his reflection in the window as the car passed a bus. His face glowed London-transport-red back at him, the military moustache a slash of white. He turned away and gazed ahead. The one o'clock news led on the potential crisis in South Lebanon and he wondered if the paper would splash on it tomorrow; the decision would no doubt depend on Paula Crosley's copy and it was a comforting thought that she was out there. Ormsby was glad that the *Register* had Paula Croxley. In the past eighteen months she had sent some memorable stuff and if

15

she didn't get next month's National Council award, then there was no justice.

The news ended and he put Paula Croxley out of his mind and concentrated on the man he was about to see. Clare had told him that there would be a story in the paper tomorrow. Bill Sutcliffe, the City Editor, was working on it: John Bennet, the favourite to take over the *Daily Mercury*; the kid from South London who had made good. Would he get the paper and, if so, which way would he take it? Would it be more tits 'n' bums, more Coronation Street exclusives, Joan Collins and Princess Di? Or would he take it up-market, attacking the *Mail*? Ormsby doubted it. Given his reputation, the paper would probably sink even deeper into the morass of mindlessness. Nonetheless he was curious to meet the man. 'Here we are sir.' The chauffeur's voice crackled through the intercom as the Bentley glided to a halt. Ormsby stepped out and walked swiftly towards the canopy, wondering if the proposition Bennet had in mind was sound. If so, then there could be a mutual advantage and it wouldn't be the first time that Frank Ormsby had done a deal with someone of whom he disapproved.

He sucked in his stomach – at least he was hungry. Whatever else happened or did not happen, he promised himself that he would kill his hangover with the lunch . . .

The first surprise was that they were not alone. Ormsby looked up at Bennet, then down at a small, ferrety little man who was chewing a bread roll and playing with the crumbs.

'Frank Ormsby,' said Bennet. 'Walter Schiff, my attorney.'

Ormsby sat down, refused a cocktail and concentrated on Schiff.

'And what exactly do you do, Mr Schiff?' he asked.

'Law,' he said – a strangulated vowel, a Brooklyn accent through the bread roll. 'Contract law.'

Ormsby turned to Bennet.

'This is an informal meeting,' he said sharply.

'Sure,' said Bennet, smiling. 'I like to see my lawyer eat. Reminds me he's human. Do you want him to leave?'

16

Schiff looked at Ormsby, hands held up, in a display of mock surrender.

'No, no,' Ormsby said, 'of course not.'

'Gee thanks,' Schiff said and reached for a second roll. Ormsby wasted no time. No sooner had they given their order, than he came straight to the point.

'This is about using our printing capacity, isn't it?'

'Of course,' Bennet said. 'If I buy the *Mercury*, I'm buying the title, not their clapped-out presses. We could print on yours during the week, keeping them running seven days.'

'The old Goss wouldn't stand it,' Ormsby said.

'You're re-equipping.'

'Are we?'

Bennet leant forward and tapped the table. 'Mr Ormsby. Fleet Street's up for sale. Nobody's going to stay in business unless they get into the new technology. Fast.'

And Schiff snapped his fingers and ordered more wine . . .

Later, thinking back on it, Ormsby realised that it was Bennet's charm that had affected him. It couldn't have been the wine. He was accustomed to keeping his mouth shut over a couple of bottles of wine, and he had had only one port – so it must have been the man's charm that had caught him off guard.

He had arranged the milk jug, the sugar bowl and the coffee pot on the table to represent a map of the planned printing sites, to show Bennet how he planned to haul the *Register* into the twentieth century.

'There'll be facsimile transmission,' he said. 'Glasgow.' He pointed to the milk jug. 'Birmingham.' The coffee-pot. Then he sat back and nodded. 'As a matter of fact we need a daily paper like the *Mercury* to make this viable.' He smiled at Bennet. 'You must have a sixth sense.'

'He has more than six,' said Schiff.

Bennet ignored him and concentrated on Ormsby. 'Of course I may not get the *Mercury*.'

'Yours is the best offer,' Ormsby said.

'If I make it.'

Ormsby said nothing, trying to conceal his surprise. Surely Bennet was the favourite. Everyone said so.

'Talks are not contracts,' said Schiff.

'The share price has skyed,' Bennet said. 'They want to improve my offer. They know I want a stake here.'

'Why?'

'Because this place is opening up at last and I want some of the action. And even though I've been in the States for ten years, I've never lost my respect for this country and its traditions.'

Ormsby looked hard at him. If he was acting, then he was a good actor.

'I want a paper here,' he continued, 'but it doesn't have to be the *Mercury*.' A waiter cleared the next table and Bennet waited until he had gone, then leant forward, elbows on the table. 'I like you, Frank. I like your style. I like your paper. Your plans . . .' He passed his hand over the china printing-presses. 'Businesswise, Frank, you don't seem British and I mean that as a compliment.'

Ormsby didn't buy the flattery. Flattery put him on his guard. He looked at the coffee-pot and the milk jug and the sugar bowl and his enthusiasm evaporated.

'What are you suggesting?' he asked.

'That I buy the *Register*,' said Bennet.

'Subject to contract,' said Schiff.

For a moment there was silence, then Ormsby slowly shook his head. 'There are only two problems here, Mr Bennet,' he said. 'I don't own the paper and it is not for sale.'

'That's not my information,' Bennet said.

Ormsby stared at him. Bennet was no longer smiling. The preliminary fencing was over. Now the jackets were off. It was time to explain the facts of life to the man.

'The *Register* has been in Lord Glenross's family for fifty years,' he said. 'And he has no intention of selling it.'

'There have been talks with Associated.'

'Talks are not contracts.'

Schiff grinned. '*Touché*,' he said and raised his coffee-cup in salute.

Again Bennet ignored him. It was as if the lawyer were not there.

'You have problems,' he said to Ormsby. 'You've lost a lot of production this year.' Again he indicated the pieces of china on the table. 'How are you going to pay for this? More borrowing?'

Ormsby said nothing. He had said enough – more than enough.

'It's the family's oil and hotels that keep the paper afloat,' Bennet continued. 'Glenross is old. What happens when he's gone? I'm looking at it from your point of view. What holding has the family given you?'

It was Schiff who answered. 'One point five per cent. Non-voting shares.'

Ormsby nodded. 'As you say. Non-voting. I own little. And I have no say.'

'Glenross will take your advice,' Bennet persisted. 'I'll give you five per cent. Voting shares. And I'll guarantee the investment in this.' He tapped the jug, then the coffee-pot, then the sugar bowl. Ormsby gazed at the table, then up at Bennet and finally at Schiff. The little man reminded him of a jackal: little pointed teeth, bright eyes, ready to taste blood.

'Thank you for lunch,' Ormsby said and pushed back his chair.

'You'll think about it?' Bennet asked.

'No, Mr Bennet, I won't think about it, because if I thought about it, I would be tempted and that would be a terrible mistake.'

'Would it?'

'You might lie to me again.'

'Again?' said Bennet.

'You said that this lunch was about using our printing capacity.' He tapped the milk jug, the printing works in

Glasgow. 'I've been indiscreet,' he said.

At this, Bennet got to his feet and glared at him and, when he spoke, his voice was acid with irritation.

'Oh, come on, Ormsby. You wouldn't have come if . . .' He pushed his chair back into the path of a waiter who was carrying coffee. The waiter tripped. Coffee was spilled. Bennet's blue suit was splashed. He cursed beneath his breath and reached for a napkin. Ormsby got to his feet and turned away, the last words thrown dismissively over his shoulder.

'I don't think we're really your sort of paper Mr Bennet,' he said, the insult delivered with a polite smile. He walked out feeling contaminated, tempted by a five per cent offer from a gutter journalist, but smugly proud that he had so quickly resisted it.

# Three

To the casual observer, the atmosphere in the newsroom was as relaxed and sedate as a library. It was a large room, open-plan, taking up the whole third floor of the building. The north-facing windows overlooked Fleet Street. Three small windows faced south over St Bride's churchyard. The reporters' desks were arranged in a grid pattern and the sub-editors had a long table stretching the length of the east wall. The News Desk and Foreign Desk occupied the south-west corner, and a partition and a corridor separated the workers from the offices of the chief executives: the Features Editor, Deputy Editor, Editor and two Associate Editors, each with their own desk, door and secretary.

It was almost deserted, too early for the tension of the deadlines. At his desk, Alan Merton, the News Editor, belched lager and sausage-meat, glanced through a wad of copy and got to his feet – a tubby man with a tie at half-mast, shirt sleeves rolled up, his gentle, almost complacent, face hiding the tension, for this was his big day. He had the front and three pages to fill and he had not yet decided on priorities.

He ambled across to the Foreign Desk, where Bill Macdonald was on the phone. Macdonald, by contrast, was a sharp dresser with an equally sharp mind and, at the moment, he was tense, fingers rubbing the pulse in his temple. Merton waited until he had put the phone down, then he perched on the desk.

'I'd like Beirut for the front, Mac,' he said.

Macdonald looked up at him. 'I'd like to find Paula, Alan.'

He tapped a sheaf of papers pinned to the wall behind him, a list of names, addresses and phone numbers. 'One staff correspondent for the whole of the Middle East,' he said wearily.

'Why not try that American stringer?' Merton suggested. 'Ed whatsit?'

'Four o'clock over there,' Macdonald said. 'He'll be pissed.'

Merton shrugged and wandered off, leaving the Foreign Editor a worried man. He was so worried about Paula that he cursed her aloud, fighting the anxiety with irritation. Macdonald knew all about the dangers of Beirut. He had lost a good friend to the madmen out there and he did not know if he could handle the guilt if anything happened to her, because he'd been the one eighteen months ago who had suggested to the Editor that she should be out there . . .

On the back bench, the talk was about the *Mercury*. Jim Fowler, the Deputy News Editor, had been drinking the previous evening in the Harrow with some of the reporters and sub-editors.

'It's terrible over there,' he was saying. 'Wailing, gnashing of teeth. You know Harvey, the chief sub?' Everyone knew Harvey. Harvey was a Jonah with an ulcer and a £40,000 mortgage who had joined the *Mercury* just as the first rumours about Bennet had surfaced. 'I remember when he went to the *Evening News*. Two months later it folded. He only has to go to a paper. He sat down at *The Times* and Murdoch walked through the door. "You, you and you," Murdoch said. "Out." Terrible blood all over the floor.'

And they all laughed, each man counting his blessings and calculating his mortgage.

At the north-east corner of the room a door opened and David Clare marched in, a small, thin man of fifty-three. He was wearing a shabby suit and a bow tie. He stood for a moment surveying the place, then strode through, feeling, as always like a shark negotiating the reefs, scattering the minnows, acknowledging the respect of the bigger fish with a nod and a wave. A shark – that was how David Clare saw himself. Once, with too much claret in him, he had made the mistake of mentioning the simile out loud, in front of Toby Greene, his number two, and now they all laughed behind his back, but he never noticed and it was a merciful ignorance.

He took the lift to the eighth floor and stepped out directly into Ormsby's office. It was a large, dark room, panelled in mahogany, the east wall dominated by a five foot by three portrait of the owner, broad-shouldered, thick-featured, and glaring. Ormsby stood by the window. He smiled at Clare, offered a drink. Clare shook his head and sat down. He knew Ormsby well. The man was trying to hide some kind of tension.

'What's wrong, Frank?'

Ormsby told him.

'Cheeky sod,' Clare said. 'He'll never get the paper while I'm Editor. He's a tit and bum merchant, Frank, and proud of it. He once said he'd put his own nipples in the paper if they sold an extra copy.'

Ormsby sighed and slumped into his seat.

'Has he a chance?' Clare asked.

'Anyone must have a chance.' He nodded at the portrait. 'You know how unpredictable he is. We'll have to bring our plans forward.'

'We're not ready to take over the paper,' Clare said.

Ormsby smiled. 'I've nearly agreed the finance for a management buy-out,' he said. 'All we're arguing about now is the size of our holding and that of the bank.'

'Then we're all right. The old bastard will never sell to Bennet if we can raise the ante.'

'It's not the money,' Ormsby said. 'It's the timing. I daren't let Bennet get in first.'

Clare shook his head, working out the possibilities. 'The thing is, without the print problems we wouldn't be vulnerable. We've had some good issues this year. Readership is up. We can't say circulation is, because there are never enough copies to circulate.'

He walked to the window and looked down. Two lorries were backing along the narrow street, laden with rolls of paper.

'What's it like in the machine-room?' he asked.

'Still edgy.'

'Maybe it's a good thing. Bennet. Bringing it to a head. Every week's a crisis.'

Ormsby nodded. 'Someone's got to tell the old man it's time to go.'

'I'm afraid that's got to be you, Frank.'

'I'm afraid it has,' Ormsby said and pulled a face. It was his responsibility and he did not like it. Clare wanted to be out of the place. He glanced at his watch. It was time for conference. As he left, he turned and saw Ormsby at the window again, staring at the black clouds, his face set in shadow. He looked to Clare like a man who was preparing for a funeral.

Half an hour later, Clare led his executives out of his office. The conference had yielded a number of possibilities: Lebanon, Northern Ireland; the Leader of the Opposition talking at his weekend home about the possibility of an autumn election; Greenpeace complaining about a discharge of nuclear waste into the Irish Sea; a body in Holland Park so far unidentified, but which was rumoured to be a top civil servant . . .

As the men filed slowly out, Clare touched Bill Sutcliffe's arm and muttered, 'Bill, Bennet might be back-pedalling on the *Mercury*.'

Sutcliffe looked surprised.

'A little bird told me,' Clare said, reaching now for the arm of Toby Greene. 'Toby,' he said. 'The review section's late, which is bad, but it means we can pull the profile on what's his name.'

'For what?' Greene asked.

'Let's do John Bennet instead. An objective assessment of the man and his works.'

24

Greene grimaced. 'Including any cases of rape and incest we happen to stumble across.'

Clare smiled. 'A rounded portrait, yes.'

'So long as I don't have to write it.'

Clare took his arm, led him out into the corridor and waited until the others were out of earshot. 'Dear Toby,' he said. 'You're not frightened are you?'

Greene shook his head and returned Clare's smile. 'Pragmatic,' he said. 'What's the point of biting the hand that might feed you.'

Clare took a step back. 'You'd never work for him would you?'

'No. Of course not. Not if I could help it.' Then he shrugged and turned to survey the newsroom. 'Yes. I might even do that. I'm thirty-five. People have started to see me as a permanent number two.' He turned back and looked down at Clare. 'You know what I feel. I want my own paper.'

Clare tapped his forearm with his left hand. 'And you'll have it Toby. You've been fantastically loyal to me. Another few years. They slip by so quickly, believe me.'

Clare smiled, trying to pacify the man, but Greene continued to glower, a big man at odds with the world. Clare looked at him and decided to let him know what was going on. There was still the element of the young reporter in him. Even at fifty-three, David Clare, Editor of the prestigious *Sunday Register*, found it difficult to keep a secret.

'As a matter of fact,' he said softly, 'and strictly between ourselves, the cheeky bugger has tried to stick his nose in here.' He grinned. 'Sub-text to profile, eh Toby?'

He winked and strode off into the heart of the newsroom. Greene stared at his back. The place was busy now, most desks occupied, reporters attacking telephones and typewriters, the build-up to the most frantic few hours of the week, the tension beginning to become almost visible.

The little pompous prick, Greene said to himself. After someone like David Clare, the likes of John Bennet would be stimulating. He could work for Bennet. He turned and looked

25

into Clare's room, at the empty chair. The leather was old and tired, just like Clare. The first thing he would do would be to get a new one. The second thing would be to open the windows . . .

Walter Schiff knocked on Bennet's door and belched unexpectedly. Lunch had given him indigestion and it wasn't the food – it was Ormsby. Schiff didn't like stuffed-shirt Limeys. He never felt at ease with them and their arrogance that was founded on nothing. Limeys belonged to history, except they didn't know it; supercilious bastards most of them, who didn't know which end was up.

There was no response to his knock, so he went in. The office seemed to be empty. He gently closed the door and walked in, then heard Bennet's voice from the bedroom. Schiff wandered to the desk and looked at a mass of papers and print-outs. A report, half hidden among the telexes, caught his eye: three words in red, guaranteed to arouse curiosity: *Private and Confidential.*

From the bedroom he could hear Bennet talking to his son. He sounded worried, asking if the kid was OK. Schiff lit a cigarette, went to the window and tried to ignore the three words in red. It wasn't easy. Walter Schiff's main fuel was curiosity. It burned on a high velocity, and all the brighter if something was private and confidential.

Behind him Bennet's voice was raised in anger. Something had happened to the kid. He'd fallen somewhere in Central Park. Schiff turned and went back to the desk: it sounded as though his boss would be on the phone for a while. He quickly pulled the report from the pile and flipped it open, his stubby fingers bruising the paper as he stared at the paragraph underlined in red.

'. . . the atherosclerosis is extensive, further reducing the blood supply to the heart. In my view an operation is inadvisable . . .'

Behind, Bennet's voice was shrill. 'For God's sake.

Arnold's a security man not a cheer-leader. What if someone had grabbed Tom . . .'

Schiff turned the page, stuffed the report back into the pile and placed his cigarette on the edge of the desk.

'Yes, I know the boy's fond of Arnold,' Bennet was saying. 'That can't be helped. Get rid of him. I'll call tomorrow.'

At the sound of the phone slamming on the cradle, Schiff jumped to his feet and knocked over a pile of papers. Bennet came in, flushed with anger and took no notice of Schiff on his knees sorting out the mess. The little man got up, smiled apologetically, and grabbed a copy of the *Register* from the pile.

'The *Mercury* I can understand,' he said, 'but this sheet makes *The Wall Street Journal* look like *Playboy*.'

Bennet looked down at him, surprised for a moment to see him, then he walked to the window. 'The *Register*'s a ticket to the club of Great Britain,' he said. 'Look at Murdoch. Started with the old *Sun*. It was dull as ditchwater in those days. There's money to be made here now that the unions are tearing themselves apart.'

He turned and looked at the film poster. 'Do you remember when Tom burned himself?' he asked.

Schiff nodded.

'Every day until she died, that bitch gave me nightmares about him.'

'I could take it down,' Schiff said. 'We could go home.'

Bennet said nothing, just stared at the poster as if hypnotised, then twitched at the sound of someone knocking, and turned to see Debbie looking in.

'Lord Glenross is not available,' she said.

Bennet glared at her. 'I don't pay you to tell me that. Get the man on the phone.' He swore softly and turned to Schiff. 'I'd forgotten what this country was like. It's easier to get through to the White House than to some stuffed peer.'

Debbie glared back at him, then turned to go and Bennet called after her.

'Close the door. Come here. I'm sorry. I'm upset, that's all. You'll get used to me. Like Walter. He knows.' He picked up a copy of *Harpers and Queen*, opened it to a fashion spread and handed it to her. 'You dress well,' he said. 'You have taste. What do you like?'

She pouted at him, uncertain what he wanted her to say, then pointed to a dress.

'All right. Order it,' he said. 'Put it on my account here.'

'But it's three hundred pounds.'

'Now get me Glenross on the phone will you?'

She smiled at him, still uncertain and went out. Bennet stared at the closed door, then slumped into his seat and looked back at the bedroom. Schiff followed his gaze and saw the photograph of Tom on the bed.

'You shouldn't get so upset,' he said.

Bennet looked up, and shrugged.

'I couldn't help seeing the medical report,' Schiff added.

'Oh, that.'

'Is it serious?'

'Yes, Walter, it is. Very serious.'

A moment later Debbie came back, smiling, pleased with herself. 'Lord Glenross is available on Monday,' she said, but the response was the opposite to what she expected.

'On Monday,' Bennet said slowly, glaring at her, 'I have talks on another deal which I will not enter into if I can set up what appears to be a more profitable deal here.' He gestured to a pile of computer print-outs. 'Now do you understand?'

Debbie shook her head. 'I'm sorry, but I'm afraid you don't understand how this country works any more, Mr Bennet,' she said, angry and rebellious.

'It doesn't work, Miss Cartwright,' he said.

She turned and jerked the door open.

'You can keep the dress,' he said.

'No thank you,' she snapped over her shoulder, then she stopped, thinking, staring out into her office. 'Lord Glenross is dining late tonight at the Reform Club with Mr Ormsby but you won't get in.' She turned, scribbled something on her pad

28

and handed it to him. 'This man is a member. He will invite you for a sort-of fee.' Bennet looked at the scrawled name. 'He's a sort-of relative,' Debbie continued. 'And rather broke you see. Don't let him drink too much.'

Bennet nodded and reached for the magazines again but she shook her head and went to the door.

'I'd rather have the money,' she said. 'If you don't mind.'

In the newsroom, the earlier lethargy had been replaced by activity as the stories came in and the back bench worried about the choices they had to make. A television set next to the News Desk showed Israeli tanks on the move, the newscaster competing for attention with the BBC World Service's pundit, who was predicting a possible invasion.

Across the room, big Mike the cartoonist was happy. He had presented his caricature of Bennet for the change in the review section and had had it accepted. It was gruesome: Bennet as a woman with sagging breasts and the caption: '*I would put my own nipples in the paper if they sold a few copies*.'

One floor below, the linotype operators were punching metal and the compositors were setting type. In the machine-room, the printers sweated beside the vast Goss rotary printing-machine. Anywhere else in the Western world, the machine would have been in a museum, being gazed at in wonder. Here, it wheezed and clanked as the rolls of newsprint shunted through the rollers, and printers coughed and sweated beer. Outside it was a cold night. In the machine-room, singlets and jeans stuck to sweating bodies. Then, at six o'clock there was a bang. The machine-minder hit the red *stop* button and the old Goss wheezed to a halt, a roll of torn and jagged paper flapping ten feet high above the derisive cheers of the printers. Ted Lamb, the supervisor, swore long and loud, and headed for the lift that would take him to the eighth floor. He knew the way by heart. He had taken it far too often, and always with bad news.

Ormsby greeted the perspiring little man with a sigh at the news he had heard all through his working life.

'We're not going to manage a full run.'

'We've got to,' Ormsby said.

'You show me how.' Lamb was as cross as a bear. He was hot. His bald scalp itched. He needed a beer badly and now Ormsby was being unreasonable again. He tried to explain. 'We've not got through the City section yet. The review section's late.'

'The review section left editorial this morning,' Ormsby said.

'They pulled something.'

'What?'

'Bloody profile or something, I don't know. No air-conditioning down there – it's like hell on a warm day. You'll get paper breaks in that atmosphere.'

Then Ormsby said something that made Lamb want to choke him.

'It was an accident then?'

'I didn't hear that, Mr Ormsby,' Lamb said, jaw thrust forward, fists clenched, ready to pounce, but Ormsby was in no mood to back off. He leant across the desk, stabbing the air with his right index finger.

'There's no point putting air-conditioning in an old plant. We'll spend the money on the new printing works.'

'For which we have, as yet, reached no agreement unless you intend putting up a barbed wire fence.'

Ormsby turned away. He had had enough. His hangover had returned. There did not seem to be one good thing to be said about life. His shoulders sagged and Lamb suddenly felt sorry for him.

'We'll do the best we can, then,' he said.

'That won't be good enough.' He turned and looked down at the little man. 'I'm talking about survival, Ted.'

'So are the printers, Mr Ormsby.' He had heard it all before. He turned and walked into the lift, leaving a smell of sweat behind him.

★ ★ ★

Five floors below, Bill Macdonald let out a whoop into the phone and silenced the chatter around him.

'Paula!'

Clare and Greene, as one, pushed back their chairs and hurried towards the Foreign Desk. Reporters looked up from their typewriters. Conversations were halted in mid-sentence.

'Fantastic story,' Macdonald said, the receiver tucked into his shoulder at his left ear as he read a page of copy, then took another from a messenger boy. 'Yeh. Just come through from the copytaker now. Don't worry, we'll just about make the first edition . . .'

Clare and Greene clustered behind him, reading over his shoulder as Macdonald continued. 'OK, so you're saying that the incident was started by a breakaway Muslim group . . . right . . . and where did Israeli and Syrian tanks come into contact? You mean they didn't know which side of the border they were on? OK, one Israeli tank and two Syrians knocked out and you saw it happen. My God, Paula . . .'

Macdonald was a happy man. His guilt and his anxiety had been replaced by exhilaration. It was moments like these that made the job a delight. It was great copy. It was exclusive. It would get Paula Foreign Reporter of the Year if there was any justice. He hung up and beamed, looked round for the Editor, but Clare had gone. He had work to do. He had to pull rank. It was time to get people enthused.

One floor below, Clare was earning his salary, talking fast to the composing room overseer. Gary Pritchett was keen to help, if possible, but there were problems . . .

'I know, Gary,' Clare said. 'It's not a remake. We'll switch the Lebanon and the Irish stories and cut Ireland to fit. The new headings will drop straight in.'

Pritchett blew bad air, looked at the page plan and nodded.

'Thank you,' Clare said. 'That's really appreciated. She did have a bit of trouble getting it.'

For the next fifteen minutes Clare followed the process

through until he had what he wanted: a damp proof of the new front page, the headline:

## LEBANON BATTLE
### Three tanks knocked out
### Syria, Israel pull back from war

And the best word of all, in seven-point Ludlow bold:

### Exclusive

With a one-inch, half-column block of Paula, looking seriously out at her readers. Clare ran upstairs into the newsroom, grinning. Passing the News Desk, he could hear Merton on the internal phone, his voice pitched high with tension.

'The literals don't matter,' he was saying. 'Let it go, let it go. It's fine.'

Then Ormsby appeared from the far corner of the room, with Ted Lamb trailing two steps behind.

Clare flapped the page at him like a flag as Ormsby approached.

'Have you seen this, Frank?' he shouted, but Ormsby was shaking his head. There was no colour in his face. He looked about seventy years old. Clare looked at him, suddenly deflated.

'How many copies have we lost?' he asked.

'The lot,' said Ormsby. 'I'm sorry. There will be no papers printed tonight.'

Paula was too exhausted to sleep now. Beside her, the big Irishman was snoring gently. She ruffled his hair and he grunted, but did not waken. She sat up and stared across the room. Moonlight, shredding through the shutters, cast a pattern on the dressing-table. She could see her copy, six pages of it, neatly stacked, and, beside it, a crumpled blue airmail letter. She tried to arrange her thoughts and sighed. There was no longer any choice. She would have to go back.

32

The big man turned over and, in his sleep, reached for her. As she snuggled down with him, she wondered how much she would miss him and how much he would miss her, and she wondered what he would say if he knew about the airmail letter. He would not approve of what she was going to do. There was too much of the Catholic in him.

The face of his watch glowed faintly a few inches from her nose. Two o'clock, which meant midnight in London. In a few hours her face would be staring out at two million breakfasts.

'Well, Paula,' she said aloud, 'at least you've gone out with a bang.'

# Four

The old man coughed, a dry rattle, as the Rolls Royce Silver Shadow glided to a stop outside the Reform Club in Pall Mall. The door was pulled open and slowly he heaved himself out into the night rain and under the shelter of the doorman's brolly. He had to stoop. He was a big man, dressed completely in black: hat, and coat, a scarf covering his chin, only the hook nose and the bright eyes visible.

'Lord Glenross,' said the doorman.

He grunted and made his way slowly up the steps, then stopped for a moment at the door to catch his breath.

'Wet,' he said.

'It is, my Lord, yes, very wet indeed, sir, yes.'

Glenross spat into a handkerchief and sniffed.

'Bloody silly conversation,' he said and lumbered into the lobby and up to the reception desk. A porter took his coat and hat and he nodded to a colleague who was sorting out the first editions of the Sunday papers. Glenross murmured a good evening, picked up the *Observer* and shuffled through the papers.

'Where's my paper?'

'Not published, my Lord,' said the head porter.

At first he did not understand. 'Has someone taken my paper?'

'It's not printed. Not published, my Lord.'

Glenross stared at him as if the man were mad, then turned away and shuffled off towards the dining-room. Mr Ormsby was already there, the porter was telling him, but, if he heard, he paid no attention. Not published. The words were just beginning to sink in.

Ten minutes later he was staring at a plate of fish in a cheese sauce, then up into Ormsby's tired face. He waved over a waiter and glowered at him.

'I can't eat this muck. Bring me a steak.'

'Yes, my Lord,' the waiter said. 'Rare?'

'Bloody. With chips.'

'Salad on the side?'

Glenross shook his head. 'I don't want to see a lettuce leaf on this table.'

Ormsby picked up a carafe of mineral water and leant towards Glenross's glass.

'Don't water it.' He gulped from his glass and held it out for a refill.

'You shouldn't,' said Ormsby.

'Of course I shouldn't. The only reason I come to this bloody place is to do what they won't let me do at home.' He guzzled more wine and belched. 'I'm going to suffer for this tomorrow, Frank, but I always have a drink on press day.'

He placed the glass on the table, his fingers shaking, spilling some, but he did not notice. He was too intent on the news he'd been given.

'Five times it hasn't appeared in a hundred years. General strike. Once in the Blitz and even then we got out a few. I remember bundling them myself. No one said you haven't a ticket to do that. Someone said, "Come on mate, we'll nevva get 'em aht." Then he saw it was me.'

He smiled, lost in the better old days.

'I tried to phone you,' Ormsby said. 'I'm sorry.'

Glenross shrugged. 'I swore I'd keep it going until it ran my obituary.' He raised his glass, silently toasted himself, then looked at Ormsby. 'How much has tonight's little episode cost me?'

'Two hundred thousand.'

The old man shook his head. 'I can't do it. You know what the situation is. I've stripped myself to avoid death duties. My sons don't want it. They hate it. Do you know what they call it? Dad's train set.' He battered his fist on the table, spilling more wine. 'It's been the best thing in my life. I love it. I even love that damned building.' He pointed to the papers. 'Put those away, Frank.'

Ormsby did as he was bid, stuffed the papers into his briefcase and stammered. 'I've . . . ah . . .'

'I've spoken to Rupert,' Glenross said suddenly. Ormsby blinked. 'Murdoch? Without telling me?'

'It is my paper.'

Ormsby nodded. 'I've put a little into it,' he said, making no attempt to hide the bitterness.

'I know, I know,' Glenross said, then looked up as his steak arrived. He poked it with his fork, ate a chip and nodded approval. 'It has more blood than I have. Have a chip, Frank. Best thing they do here.' He looked up at the waiter. 'Tell him the chips are superb.' Then he turned back to Ormsby. 'What else can I do?' he said. 'Rupert's behaving himself. He hasn't put tits in *The Times* yet. He's almost one of us now.'

Ormsby shook his head. 'He doesn't want another Sunday. He'll kill it.'

'He'll keep our title in *The Sunday Times* masthead. Some of our features. Some of our writers.'

'For how long?' Ormsby asked, then tapped his chest. 'I'd be out.'

Glenross sagged in his chair and let his knife and fork slip onto his plate. 'I'm tired, Frank. I've had enough.'

But Ormsby would not let up. He looked at Glenross and was reminded of the portrait. It had always reminded him of the stag at bay and now the old stag was cornered and exhausted, and Ormsby went for the throat.

'Did it never occur to you that I might be interested?'

'You?' Glenross gaped at him. 'You haven't any money, Frank.'

'I don't have to have a great deal.'

Glenross folded his arms and squinted at him. 'I'd like to give it to you Frank but . . .'

36

'We'll pay the market price,' Ormsby said quickly. 'I've been talking to Pioneer. They provide venture capital. They would take an eighty per cent holding and Clare and I would have twenty. You know we would keep it according to your wishes.'

'Would you? Well, well. The world changes. You and David. Interesting. And you can raise all that money?'

Ormsby nodded, then sat up straight, startled. While they had been talking, three tables had emptied, and, in the corner, he saw the last person he expected to find in the club. Bennet caught his eye and waved at him. Walter Schiff smiled. A third man nodded. Ormsby vaguely knew him, a member of the club, a county type, down on his luck. 'What sort of money, Frank?' Glenross was saying. 'What's the matter? Who the devil are you staring at?'

Ormsby told him and Glenross grinned, reminding Ormsby of a gargoyle; in his youth the grin would probably have been described as mischievous. Now it looked evil.

Before their meal ended, Bennet's third man had taken his leave and Bennet and Schiff had moved off in the direction of the library.

Glenross gave them five minutes, then struggled to his feet and followed them, Ormsby a step behind. They reached the door and saw the two men, again in the far corner, coffee and brandies on a table between them.

'Will you promise me . . .' Ormsby said as the old man lurched towards them.

'Frank,' he said, 'I'm old, but not yet senile. Nothing would induce me to sell to that jumped-up guttersnipe, but the more bidders, the higher the price.'

Ormsby moved in front of him as Bennet and Schiff got to their feet. He fixed a smile and made the introductions. Glenross immediately took charge. He was on home territory and comfortable and, besides, he was the one who owned the product. He permitted a couple of minutes of small talk, then leant back and squinted at Bennet.

'Who told you my paper is for sale?'

'Is it?' Bennet asked.

'It might be. It might not be. I don't know. It's a responsibility. A curse. A drain. A bloody nuisance.' He reached for his glass, sipped and grimaced. 'That's not my brandy, Frank. Tell them it's not my brandy.' Then he looked back at Bennet. 'Why the hell do you want it?' he asked, jaw pushed forward, belligerent, a question like a left hook to the liver.

'Because I'm a guttersnipe,' Bennet said.

'What?' He looked at Ormsby. 'What did he say?'

Ormsby smiled at Bennet, enjoying himself for the first time that day. 'I'm sorry. Lord Glenross is upset. Losing the issue . . .'

'Don't apologise for me,' Glenross snapped, glaring at Bennet. 'I heard what he said. I've read your American papers. Pretty poisonous stuff.'

Schiff butted in with a smile, 'They cater for a market.'

Ormsby fielded the remark. 'Or create one,' he suggested.

For a moment there was a silence; a stand-off, then a waiter arrived with a brandy glass. Glenross took it and sniffed it.

'Full of sex and violence,' he said.

'Like the *Register*,' said Bennet.

Ormsby and Glenross looked at one another and laughed, but Bennet wasn't making jokes. He was angry and fighting to control his temper. 'Only it uses longer words,' he continued, 'like love and conflict.'

Glenross smiled benignly at him. For a moment Ormsby thought the old man was going to lean forward and pat Bennet's head, like a puppy. Instead Bennet got to his feet and glared down at them.

'There are only two types of newspaper: winners and losers,' he said, then looked to his left. Standing, he could see Ormsby's briefcase. It was open. The proof of the front page stuck out – Paula's picture and her exclusive story.

'That's where we differ, you see,' Glenross said, his smile still intact. 'We're taught at school that winning isn't important.'

38

'Sod that,' said Bennet, turning to the window and pointing. 'The losers are out there.' He was almost shouting. He had broken an elementary rule of behaviour. People turned to look at him. He sat down and apologised.

For a moment there was silence. Glenross lit a cigar and quietly savoured his small victory. Bennet had shown emotion and showing emotion was a lack of breeding. Now was the right time to tell him the facts of life.

'The *Register* is an institution, Mr Bennet,' he explained slowly and carefully, talking as if to a child. 'You know nothing about this country. You live in America.'

'I lived here till I was thirty,' Bennet said.

'Ah yes. And what did your father do?'

'He was killed in the Battle of Britain.'

Glenross was about to sip his brandy. The glass hovered at his lips.

'He loved this country,' Bennet continued. 'He was a *Register* reader.' He smiled and held out his hand towards the briefcase. 'May I?'

Ormsby leant down and passed him the proof of the front page. Bennet scanned it and nodded. 'Great story,' he said.

'I found Paula,' Glenross said. 'I'm as fond of her as I am of my own children.' He paused. 'Fonder, in fact.'

'Your sons don't like newspapers?'

The question made Glenross smile. Bennet leant forward to tuck the proof into the briefcase and saw a caricature of himself: a crushed, crumpled figure with a woman's body — ugly breasts and a caption about nipples.

'I still don't think you understand, Mr Bennet,' Glenross said. 'The *Register* is more than a newspaper — it's a public responsibility. It's mine, but not mine to dispose of, do you see?' He pointed his cigar at Ormsby's chest. 'He wants it. Rupert wants it. Others will be no less eager to take this incubus from me. If I tried to sell the paper to you, my family and fellow directors would look askance. The government would probably block it. The staff wouldn't stand for it and the unions would be up in arms.' He took a long pull at his cigar, blew smoke at the ceiling and watched it rise. 'What would you offer?' he asked.

Bennet smiled and got to his feet. The question could be taken two ways. What would you offer the paper? Or: what would you offer to buy the paper? Either way, it was not the time to give an answer. He left with a quiet 'good-night' thrown over his shoulder and Schiff followed like an obedient puppy.

They stepped into Pall Mall, shoulders hunched against the night air. Schiff beckoned to the doorman for a taxi but Bennet was already walking westwards.

'We'll walk. I need air,' he said.

Walk? Schiff thought. It was a mile maybe. Who needed to walk. He scampered after him and caught up. 'Take it easy,' he said. 'No paper's worth a heart attack.'

'What?' Bennet said. 'I nearly had one in there.'

'He's using you,' Schiff said. 'Playing you off against . . .'

'I know what he's doing,' Bennet said angrily. 'I should have had him. I could have had it cheap.'

'How?'

'I ballsed it up. I shouldn't have lost my temper. I played it all wrong.'

He was walking fast, head down into the wind, and Schiff had to trot to keep up with him. Then a fragment of the conversation surfaced, something Bennet had said that surprised him.

'Hey,' he said. 'I didn't know your father was in the Battle of Britain.'

'He wasn't. He was court-martialled. Lost his nerve. He wouldn't fly. They broke him. Bastards like that. That's why I'm going to beat them.'

Schiff grinned. He was on sure ground again. Revenge he understood.

'So let's beat the schmucks,' he said. 'So long as there's a profit in it.'

Bennet grinned down at him. 'Good old Walter,' he said. 'Keep me on the straight and narrow.'

40

A taxi came towards them with its light on. Bennet hailed it and they clambered into the back. The little man wheezed and sat back, panting from the walk, thinking aloud.

'He probably won't sell it to anyone,' he said. 'You know these old men who won't let go.'

'He's got to let go,' Bennet said. 'That's why there isn't much time.' Bennet squinted at Schiff, thinking back to something he had said. 'You didn't really think that medical report was mine, did you?'

Schiff shrugged.

'I got it from a private eye. Not a doctor.'

The cab stopped outside the hotel and Schiff scrabbled in his pocket for change.

'Glenross is dying,' Bennet said. 'He's got two months. If that.'

# Five

For almost a month Frank Ormsby had watched himself ageing. Each morning his mirror seemed to reflect an older face. What he desperately needed was an answer – even the wrong answer would be better than this appalling hiatus, but the old man would not be hurried. He was virtually uncontactable. He wouldn't answer the phone. Letters went unanswered. Rumour had it that he was planning to move into his club where he would be even further shielded from intrusion. And, what was worse, the money men were stalling.

The *Standard* lay on his desk that morning, the early edition leading on the battle, the headline seeming to mock him: *Fight for Register: Bennet Ups Offer £1 Million* followed by the story of Bennet meeting strong opposition from the management buy-out attempt by himself and David Clare.

Clare stood now with his back to the window as Ormsby tried to get some decision from his backers.

'Tom, we can beat Bennet,' he said. 'Glenross wants to sell to us but he must be sure we have the working capital.'

He looked up at Clare, who grinned back at him and held up both hands, his fingers crossed.

'Yes, Tom,' Ormsby continued, trying to remain calm, forcing the pleading tone from his voice. 'The new shares will bring in five million but he wants a guarantee from you . . .' He paused while the other man complained. 'There's no time for discussion,' he added. 'He might go at any minute.'

He waited for a moment – silence at the other end of the line. His extension rang. Clare picked it up and mouthed to him that Lady Glenross was on her way up. Ormsby nodded, felt the perspiration run down his right arm, then the man on the other line said something that took ten years off him. The furrows softened. He smiled, gave the thumbs up to Clare. 'Thank you, Tom, that's wonderful.' Clare strode towards them and the two men clasped hands. 'Can you let me have that in writing and bike it round? Of course I trust you, but Glenross doesn't trust anyone. Thanks a million, Tom, as it were.' He dropped the phone and raised his fist in a gesture of victory. 'David,' he said. 'We've got it. We've got the money.'

The door opened as they were hugging each other and they turned to see a tall woman walk in. Lady Glenross was wearing a black evening dress and an ankle-length coat. She was thin – too thin, Ormsby thought – and pale with exhaustion.

'Joyce,' said Ormsby. 'What happened? How is he?'

'I've no idea,' she said. 'He hasn't been home for three days,' and she smiled, but it was a forced smile. She was being brave, but the dark smudges beneath her eyes gave a hint of sleepless nights.

'Where is he?' Clare asked.

'At his club. He's going to the party tonight. At least, that's what the club tells me. They keep me informed. They don't want him to die there.'

She moved away to the window and Ormsby went to her. It was well known that Glenross gave his wife a hard time. He was an awkward character, the kind who inspire legend and lounge-bar gossip, but who are impossible to live with.

'Sometimes,' she said to the window, 'I think I'll just leave him to it.' Then she turned and smiled again. 'He threw tea at his doctor. He's been to see some quack who says he's going to live to a hundred.'

Clare poured her a glass of brandy and she sipped it, then sighed. 'If only we could settle on the sale of the paper . . .'

'We've raised all the money,' Ormsby said.

She lowered her glass and nodded.

43

'Your sons are not in favour of our bid,' Clare said.

'I am,' she said.

'Thank you,' said Ormsby.

'And, with my husband, we have two-thirds of the voting shares, which should be sufficient. He'll never sell to Bennet. He's putting you through it as he puts me through it.' She put down her glass and moved to the door. 'Will you go and see him, Frank?'

Ormsby nodded. 'Of course.' And all three looked at the contract on the desk. It was neatly typed. It was bound in blue. There was money to back it up. All that was needed was the old man's signature . . .

An hour later, the contract lay on a coffee table in the library of the Reform Club. Glenross flipped a page, looked up at Ormsby, then at the ceiling. For a full minute he said nothing and Ormsby felt himself ageing again.

'New issue,' he said at last. 'The money is only on paper.'

Ormsby reached into his jacket pocket and flapped an envelope in front of his face like a fan, wafting away the cigar smoke. 'It's guaranteed,' he said. 'That's as good as cash.'

Glenross nodded. 'I'll see my lawyers in the morning.'

It wasn't the answer Ormsby wanted. Months of frustration exploded into an angry outburst. 'Are you going to sell me the paper or not? You can't sell it to that man.'

'I'll sell it to whom I choose.'

Ormsby got to his feet. He had had enough. It was unfair. What was it about the imminence of death that made men like Glenross terminally stubborn? He felt like reaching for the old throat with both hands, speed up the process, choke a signature out of the old bastard.

'Sit down, Frank,' Glenross said softly. Ormsby sighed and shook his head. It was a small mutiny, a tiny fit of pique but the hell with it, he thought. He'd had a lifetime of sitting opposite Glenross, choking on brandy fumes and cigar smoke.

Glenross continued, conciliatory now, avuncular, soothing the other man's temper – stubborn at first, then reasonable, hard and soft in equal measure; it was an ancient ploy and Ormsby wasn't buying.

'I must be sure the *Register* is left in the right hands, Frank, although I shall, of course . . . what is the vogue phrase . . .? positively discriminate towards your bid.'

'Thank you.' Two syllables like icicles, freezing the atmosphere.

'On the other hand,' Glenross said and smiled. 'I may not sell at all.' It was mischief – an old man pulling the wings off butterflies. Ormsby shook his head.

'You can't keep it going,' he said.

'It's wonderful how a recovery in health can make one reassess one's resources. I feel a new man. Homeopathy, and coming to live at my club. No more fish, or salad, or family fuss. I haven't felt like this since I left my first wife.' He held out his hand, fingers extended and, for a moment, Ormsby thought he was being asked to kiss the old man's signet ring. 'Is my pulse fluttering? Feel it, Frank. Steady as a rock.' Ormsby reached for the wrist and nodded dutifully. 'Now. Give me a hand up.'

'I don't think you should go tonight.'

'Nonsense.' He stared at Ormsby, breathing brandy. 'Have you seen Joyce?'

'No.'

Glenross grinned. 'You're lying. You're a good man, Frank. I'm very fond of you.' He reached over and tapped the contract. 'You don't know whether to please Joyce or please me, do you? Now give me a hand up.'

It was true, Ormsby thought. The stubborn old fool was all set for a night on the town.


They'd all told her she looked terrific, the men genuine, some of the women less so, but Paula was not convinced. The dress was three years old and too tight. Kath, her sister, had let out a seam for her so that it more or less fitted, but maybe she was showing too much cleavage. Maybe, when the time came, the old devil would look down the front of her dress and they'd be

45

on the front pages next morning with leery captions . . .

'More wine?' Toby Greene asked.

She nodded, tense with excitement and pride, and fear that maybe she would make a fool of herself. The ballroom of the Dorchester was packed with friends and enemies, politicians and TV people, and she'd never had to do this before. This was her first award, apart from the old days when she'd got that provincial Journalist of the Year thing; but this was another level altogether. Foreign Reporter of the Year. They all said she deserved it – Bill, Clare, Greene, Ormsby – but then they would, wouldn't they? Since she'd been told, she had tried to appear blasé and humble, but deep down she was pleased with herself. She *did* deserve it. She'd had a good year and she was determined to enjoy herself tonight because she had no idea what she would be doing tomorrow . . .

'Top up?' Bill said, and again she nodded. She was drinking too quickly, but the hell with it. She needed Dutch courage.

Ten feet away, Lord Wilson was on his feet and enjoying himself.

'. . . then there was the General who reflected one view of war correspondents. He said: "I wouldn't tell the people anything until the war was over. Then I'd tell them who won." '

All round the room faces crackled with laughter. People thumped tables in appreciation. Lord Wilson smiled. Paula tried a grin but it came out as a grimace. She'd heard the story before and she was too nervous to laugh.

Lord Wilson waited for the applause to die down. Paula, watching him, could understand why he was so relaxed. People were laughing along with him. It wasn't like the House, where, as often as not, he had to wait until the baying of the Opposition had died down before he could continue.

'You,' he continued, 'I believe, have a slightly different attitude.' He paused. 'Fortunately.' Paula glanced at Lord Glenross. The old man was nodding agreement. 'Ladies and gentlemen,' Lord Wilson said, 'as every member of the

House of Commons, and indeed the Lords, knows, democracy is nurtured on information.'

A murmur of agreement. He waited until it died down, then continued. 'In war situations it depends on brave people risking their lives to tell the truth as they see it.'

Paula blinked, looked at the tablecloth, feeling proud, embarrassed and slightly silly all at once and hoping to God she wouldn't get the goddam hiccups. Lord Wilson reached for a plaque.

'The next award goes to such a person, whose outstanding coverage of the Middle East we have all read with such admiration. Paula Croxley of the *Sunday Register*.'

She took a deep breath and got to her feet, the applause battering her eardrums. One step and she stumbled against Clare's chair. He half got up and held out a hand to steady her, then she was moving forward, feeling like a fighter on his way to the ring. Faces, known and unknown, grinned up at her; she felt someone's hand on her back, patting. Then she was at the top table and Glenross was holding out his arms to her and beaming. She bent and kissed him. There was a roar of approval, then she was in the glare of the TV cameras and Lord Wilson was reaching out his hand in congratulation.

Throughout the evening Bennet had drunk little, sitting at the corner table watching the guests. The band was playing a Beatles melody and, for a moment, he watched the red-head who'd won the award dancing with her Editor. She was flushed and animated. Half pissed, he reckoned. Then he saw Schiff battling his way across the dance floor towards him. Bennet turned to the man who had been sitting next to him for the past ten minutes.

'Walter Schiff, my lawyer. Toby Greene. Toby is Deputy Editor of the *Register*.'

Schiff shook hands and sat down. 'Are the journalists seeing sense?' he asked.

'You mean, your sense?' Greene said.

'Sure.'

47

Greene shrugged. 'About half are in favour of Mr Bennet's bid. I am. So is Sutcliffe, the City Editor.' Sutcliffe was dancing a few feet away and wearing a paper hat. He turned, as if hearing his name, and waved. 'More would come out,' Greene continued, 'if they weren't frightened.'

'Of what?' asked Bennet.

'You.'

Bennet grinned. 'I drink blood?'

'They think you'll interfere.'

'I'll only interfere one way editorially,' he said, and turned to look at the dance floor, at Clare dancing with Lady Glenross. 'If I walk in, the present Editor walks out.'

'I think I could come to terms with that,' Greene said. 'But what happens if the old bastard won't sell?'

'He'll sell,' said Bennet, turning again to look at the top table where Glenross was holding court, the table laughing along with his story.

'I know him,' Greene continued. 'He'll keep his hands on the bloody paper until he runs out of money or dies.'

'Then what would happen?' Schiff asked.

'His wife will get it.'

'How do you know?' Schiff asked again.

'Clare told me. If he kicks it, Ormsby gets the paper and . . .'

Bennet leant towards him, one hand outstretched, urgent. 'Give me your cummerbund.'

Greene blinked in surprise.

'Quick.'

Greene did not argue, did not stop to ask what all this was about. He unwrapped the piece of silk, handed it to Bennet and watched him move quickly across the floor to the bandstand where Paula was standing, her arms tight around her waist, her face bright with embarrassment. Something had split. The Foreign Reporter of the Year was bulging at the seams. Greene watched Bennet produce the cummerbund, saw Paula stammer thanks, then rush off with it towards the cloakrooms. Greene smiled. Bennet to the

48

rescue. In the nick of time – but somehow the role of gallant knight did not quite rest easily with him . . .


By midnight Paula was relaxed. As relaxed as a newt, she told herself, mashing a cigarette into an ashtray that resembled a bomb site. Somewhere among the rubble of glasses was her brandy. She tried to find it. The clue was her lipstick smeared on the rim, but she wasn't sure. She picked up the nearest glass and took a gulp. Somewhere, nearby, at the same table, a tall, rather attractive, stranger was paying her a compliment, something about her piece on the women of Iran.

'Funny,' she said.

'What?' said the tall man.

'You're the only person here who's actually talked about what I've written.' The man was handing over a glass with a lipstick smear. 'Thanks,' she said and focused on him. 'I haven't met you before.'

'No.'

'I know your face. I'm so drunk. Are you in newspapers?'

'In a small way,' he said, then began the compliments again, saying her work hadn't got the prominence it deserved.

'Foreign stuff,' she said, grimacing into the bottom of her glass. 'Editors don't like it.' She smiled at him. 'The *Register* loves me tonight, but not when I put in my expenses. Anyway, I expect I'll soon be chopped.'

'Why?'

'We're being taken over. Ormsby, Murdoch or the other man.' She shook her head, trying to think of a name. 'Some moronic millionaire who thinks with his testicles. Foreign coverage will be out. Tits in. I couldn't work for a bastard like that. Might pack it in anyway. I've no control over what I write. How it's used. Whether it's used.' Then she stopped and sat forward, elbows on the table, hands on her chin. 'Oh dear,' she said. 'I'm telling my innermost secrets to a complete stranger.'

'You haven't told me anything yet.'

'I'm pregnant,' she said and laughed. 'It's never happened to me before. I'm not married. I'm thirty-six. I'm terrified.'

'Who's the lucky man?'

'He doesn't know. He's the nicest man in the whole world. He's somewhere in Beirut. Some days I love him.'

'Are you going to have it?'

'Well, that's it, you see. I came here to decide, well, to get this award, to think about Life, you know. Life, the purpose of, existence. Slow down the world, do I want to get off, the sort of thoughts most people have as teenagers. You see me standing, sitting at crossroads . . .'

The band began to play 'Auld Lang Syne' and Paula looked up to see a scrum of men and women bearing down on her, Glenross in the lead. 'Oh hell,' she said. 'My paper. Help me please.'

She could not move. She wanted to stand, but her legs were not answering the messages from her brain.

'Join-hands-time, Paula,' said Clare.

She smiled and heard Greene making introductions, pushing Clare forward towards the tall man.

'Do you know John Bennet, David? David Clare.'

John Bennet. That was the name. The man who thinks with his testicles.

'Oh God,' Paula grunted. 'Oh no . . .'

Then she was being half dragged onto the floor by Glenross, his lips at her ear. 'Haven't held your hand all evening. You're so warm, so lovely. Give me a cuddle. Still capable you know. Still capable.'

Beneath the cummerbund, the seam gave another couple of inches and she found herself in a circle, Glenross on one side of her, Ormsby on the other, that terrible dirge: *Should auld acquaintance be forgot*, like it was New Year, the man with the testicles singing, Lady Glenross trying to get to them, but held back by the crush; then they were dancing forward, half staggering, bumping into people: *We'll drink a cup of kindness yet*, a dead weight beside her, dragging her down, her seam splitting again and she turned and looked down at Glenross

50

on his knees, his face like a balloon, eyes staring, breath rasping, then Ormsby was at his side, ripping the tie away from the collar and the others still singing, unaware of the man dying in their midst.

# Six

David Clare's desk was cluttered with the morning papers. The collapse of Glenross had made the final editions with the hospital statement that his condition was critical.

'An era has ended . . .' Clare said to the ceiling as he stretched out in his chair. Ellie, his secretary, wrote down the phrase and looked up, waiting.

'. . . with the death of Charles John Leicester, Lord Glenross.' He sniffed and glanced at her. 'Does that sound too portentous?'

Ellie shrugged – hadn't a clue what portentous meant.

'I don't think so,' Clare answered himself and picked up a couple of sheets of copy. 'Toby's obit. is a mite prosaic,' he said, then continued to gaze at the ceiling as if in search of inspiration. 'A disciple of Northcliffe, a dedicated opponent and friend of Beaverbrook, he was the last of the old press barons. Paragraph.

'During the war he was a senior adviser to the Ministry of Information . . .' He closed his eyes and wondered how the campaign was going, a few yards away in the newsroom. Alan Merton would be seeking support for the takeover and he wondered how many would sign, how many would remain loyal to him and Ormsby, how many would hold off in case Bennet and Greene attempted some last-minute skulduggery. He opened his eyes and looked across at Ellie, with that inquiring gaze she knew well.

'Senior adviser to the Ministry of Information . . .' she prompted.

'Right.'

Fifteen minutes later he emerged with his copy, crossed the newsroom to Greene's desk and laid it in front of him.

'Would you cast your eye over that, Toby? It's a little purple in places but then, he was rather over the top himself.'

'Is.'

'What?'

'He's not dead yet.'

'Bar the shouting, Toby. Lady Glenross told me he's unlikely to regain consciousness.' He smiled and looked down at the top of Greene's head. He was going bald. Clare smiled. 'She's a hundred per cent with us.'

Greene looked up from the copy. 'The sons aren't,' he said.

'Irrelevant, since his voting shares will pass to her.' He leant forward and spoke softly. 'I don't bear grudges, Toby.'

Greene frowned. 'What does that mean?'

'You can stay on.'

'You mean you can't get the paper out without me.' He shook his head. Two men nearby were trying hard to appear not to listen. 'I shall leave,' he said.

Clare smiled and laid a photograph of Glenross on the desk. 'This one, do you think? Typical of the old rogue. Across three columns.'

He smiled, turned and went back to his office and checked his watch. Ormsby was due in half an hour with the contract. He shivered with apprehension. He could hardly wait. Soon it would all be over . . .


Ormsby arrived early, the contract in his briefcase. He took it out and looked closely at Clare. The man was almost salivating, like some hound in sight of a bone. Ormsby tossed it to him, then turned to the last page where spaces were reserved for signatures.

'Joyce can't sign until the will is proved,' he said.

'How long will that take?'

Ormsby was about to answer, when there was a knock on the door and Greene came in. He was clutching a page proof,

53

the word *obituary* prominent in capitals.

Clare took it and thanked him.

'Can I see you?' Greene asked.

'After conference.'

Greene nodded, turned to go, then stopped as the intercom buzzed and Ellie's voice announced that Lady Glenross was on the line. He stopped and turned, watched Clare pick up the phone.

'Joyce?' Clare said. He listened for a moment, then sat down hard, the pulse in his temple throbbing. 'Good heavens,' he said. 'That's unexpected . . . yes, good news. What an amazing constitution . . .' He looked up at Ormsby, who snatched up the contract and stuffed it back into his briefcase.

'What?' Clare said. 'Yes of course. We'll be right over.'

He put the phone down and stared at the others. He had gone pale. 'He's rallied,' he said. 'He wants an editorial conference in the hospital.'

'Conference?' Ormsby repeated.

'Conference,' said Clare. 'On the invasion of France.'

Greene fought to hide a smile, then stood back as Clare and Ormsby left. He watched them go, then folded the obituary, picked up the phone and dialled.

'John Bennet, please,' he said, the smile widening now – a happy man and almost triumphant.

It had been a long day and Paula was exhausted. The hangover from the awards' party had lingered and she had had to leave the old man's side every half an hour to get coffee, and each time she thought he might have given up the struggle. She looked back and smiled at Lady Glenross, and at the old man, asleep now, white-faced, hands clasped over his stomach, the drip in his arm and the oxygen bottle by his bed. Then she closed the door and went out into the corridor, wondering if she would see him again.

She looked up and saw Clare and Ormsby striding towards her. Vultures, she thought. It had been difficult not to laugh

54

earlier in the day when they had sat by the old man's side pretending to take him seriously as he rambled about the invasion.

Now Clare was chuckling. 'Who should I be, Frank?' she heard him say. 'Winston? Monty?'

'That's not funny,' Paula said as they reached her. 'He's perfectly lucid now, you'll be sorry to hear.'

Ormsby shook his head. 'I'm sorry he's dying, Paula, but I don't want the paper to go with him.'

She pushed past them, heels clicking on linoleum.

'I expect he'll go on Saturday night,' Clare was saying. 'Just after we've gone to press.'

Paula pushed open the doors into the night. If it hadn't been a hospital, she would have slammed them. Tired, angry, hungover, she reached her car and slipped the key into the lock, then twitched, startled, as she felt a hand on her arm. She turned to see Bennet looking at her.

'How is he?' he asked.

'Alive.' She turned away from him and opened the door. 'You're not interested in how he is.'

'On the contrary.'

'Excuse me,' she said.

'Can we talk?'

'I have to go.'

'Five minutes,' he insisted.

She got into the car and looked up at him, at his anxious face. Maybe the man was concerned about Glenross. Who was she to judge?

'I'm sorry,' she said. 'I'm sorry about last night. Is that what you want to hear? I was drunk. I didn't know what I was saying.'

'You seemed to know exactly what you were saying.'

She tried to close the door but he leant inside and took her arm.

'Please,' she said. 'I'm tired . . .'

'We can go to . . .'

She had had enough. She didn't need this man with his

sewer mind, grappling with her in her own car. She squirmed away and slammed the door, heard it close on his hand, heard him curse.

She opened the door again and looked up at him, saw the pain and anger, then she pointed to a signpost at the car-park exit.

'There's a casualty department here,' she said, then switched on the ignition and drove off, leaving him clutching his fingers and glaring after her.

It was a five-mile drive to her flat, to coffee and bed. With luck she would be asleep before her head hit the pillow. She yawned, then blinked as she saw headlights flashing in her mirror. She ignored them. There was a red light ahead. She slowed and stopped, then glanced to her left as a black car careered alongside her, then turned fast, tyres squealing, to stop broadside on in front of her.

Bennet got out and came towards her. The hell with him, she thought, spitting angry now, her lethargy turning to temper. She jumped out of the car and glared at him.

'I only wanted to ask you . . .' he said.

'What the bloody hell do you think you're doing?'

'Would you be Editor?'

She gaped at him. The lights turned to green and the hooting of car horns began, a discordant cacophony, lights flashing at them.

'Editor!' she said, dumbly.

'Of the *Register.*'

And she sat on the bonnet of her car and began to laugh.

The pub was a dump. Wallpaper peeled. The lavatories smelled. The juke-box blared discordant guitars. Noisy young men played pool and darts and swore all the time, but Paula was only vaguely aware of the place. She was trying to concentrate on what Bennet was saying. He was crazy. She told him so. For a start he did not even own the paper. He had no chance of owning the paper.

'Then why are you here?' he asked.

'Because you nearly ran me down.'

It was a cop-out of an answer and they both knew it.

'You can always go,' he said.

He was right. She looked around the pub, then back at Bennet, a man in a five-hundred-dollar suit eating a couple of fifty-pence sausages. There was only one reason he was making his proposal.

'I know what you want,' she said. 'You know I get on with the old man. He always goes on about how he found me. I was a secretary in his office. I desperately wanted to be a journalist. He said I wasn't one. I hadn't the right instincts. I had to resign before he gave me a chance.'

She drifted back fifteen years. The apprenticeship in Bedfordshire, years of it, then back to the *Register*, no longer a secretary.

'His discovery,' Bennet said. 'His daughter – doesn't he call you that?'

She watched him munch into his second sausage and wondered if he knew what kind of garbage he was eating, or if he cared.

'You're just using me,' she said. It was obvious. He nodded.

'Of course. As you would be using me. We all use each other. It's the only way things get done.'

She looked at him and was reminded of the first man who had proposed to her. Like this place, it was an unlikely setting: a snooker hall, an executive on the paper running away from his wife and offering marriage to her. It had been sad and ludicrous at the same time. This was only ludicrous. It was time to explain the facts to this character.

'I couldn't do the job even if I wanted it, which I don't. I'm a reporter, not an editor. I hate being inside. I'm not interested in the bloody paper. I don't even know if I'm interested in journalism any more.'

She turned away from him, wondering what it was about him that made her confess to him; maybe he had been trained in the priesthood – twice in twenty-four hours she was laying her feelings open to him. Then she thought of Glenross, with the drip in his arm and the oxygen at his side, and Clare's sick little jokes.

'You disgust me,' she said quietly. 'All of you. Why don't you leave him alone and let him die in peace?' Then she surprised herself by her next sentence. 'There's never been a woman editor in Fleet Street. Not this century,' she added, remembering some amazing Victorian woman who bought *The Sunday Times* for £11,000 in 1893 and edited it for four years. She spoke without thought, as if part of her was accepting what he was trying to offer, as if her ambition, normally repressed, had sabotaged her, escaping like some malevolent genie from a bottle.

She looked at him. He had said nothing. He just sat there, eating, waiting for her to continue.

'Do you want another drink?' she said.

He shook his head. It was time to go, to leave him with his half-eaten sausage and his crazy ideas, but, like the night before, her legs wouldn't work.

'You'd throw me out as soon as you'd got what you wanted,' she said.

'Are you asking for a contract?'

Suddenly she felt silly, wondering why she had allowed herself to be brought to this dreadful place. The pool players were swearing in harmony, Madonna screeched from the juke-box and it was past her bedtime.

'This is absurd,' she said. 'How can you offer a contract for a newspaper you don't own, to someone who isn't an editor?' There was no answer to that. Then she added a rider because she was sick of him and sick of all the intrigue. 'I wouldn't work for you anyway.'

He sat back and looked at her for a moment, then spoke quietly. 'Have you seen any of my papers?' He didn't wait for a response. 'Sure, they're mainly crap, but have you seen them?' Again, he did not wait for an answer. 'We get a bad press because we're successful, because we dig dirt and throw mud, and that's what this sanctimonious secret British society needs.' His tone of voice had remained calm. Only the meaning was violent. 'I know you're not an editor,' he continued. 'I'm giving you a chance to be one.' He caught the look of disbelief, the slight curl of the upper lip. 'I'm not doing you a favour. I'm just recognising what other people are too stupid to see. Including yourself. You think you've done very well, but your talent has been wasted, buried in the middle of the bloody desert.'

She looked away from him to the pool table, and saw the telephone door open again and Ian smiling at her.

'I'd give you the *Register*,' Bennet said, '– a free hand. You'd be a double outsider – a woman and a reporter. That would shake up the bastards.'

She looked at him, wondering what had caused him to be so bitter, and trying to fight against the feelings that his words had brought to the surface; she had always been ambitious, but it had been drummed into her that her kind of ambition wasn't quite healthy. She looked at him, and he smiled, and it was a wicked smile.

'What do you say?'

Nothing, was the answer. She got up and went to the phone. When she came back, he had gone. She found him in the car-park, staring at the sky.

'Well?' he said.

'They've told his wife to stay the night.'

'Then you'd better get over there.'

'Me?' she said.

'If he saw me, it might finish him off.'

'I can't do that,' she said, trying to sound fierce, but her voice broke and she sounded like a little girl.

'Jesus Christ,' he snapped. 'Come on. What's the matter with you?'

She shook her head. The night air had sobered her. He was no longer wickedly charming – just a tall man with wind in his hair and a smudge of sausage-meat at the corner of his mouth.

'This isn't me,' she said. 'Even if I saw him, I couldn't face the staff. Ormsby. Clare.'

59

'Clare's dead wood,' he said. 'And if you're going to be capable of doing anything big, you have to clear it. Ormsby's a pity. They wouldn't last a year. They haven't the money. Some of the staff already see that. They'll accept you.'

'Stabbing Ormsby in the back,' she said.

'Saving their jobs.'

She turned and looked at him, but now it was he who had had enough.

'Do it or don't do it,' he said, a hint of weariness in his voice. He reached into his pocket, took out his wallet, drew out a business card and handed it to her. 'If you don't do it, I haven't missed anything. I'm at this number. Schiff is there. He has the contracts drawn up.'

She took it, and watched him get into his car and drive off without so much as a good-night, then she looked at the card and found she was trembling. She was a mess, five feet six of conflicting emotions, but already she knew which part of herself she was going to indulge.

Fifteen minutes later she was back in the hospital and heading for the private rooms. Lady Glenross got to her feet as she tiptoed in.

'How is he?' Paula whispered.

'A bit better. Better enough to be terribly upset.'

'Why?'

'He's just read his obituary. Somehow a proof got among the cards.'

The woman looked exhausted and Paula hugged her, whispered to her, trying to comfort her, then the old man stirred.

'Who's that? Reggie?'

His wife put her finger to his lips, but he twisted away. 'Don't shush me, woman,' he grumbled, then saw Paula and beckoned her over.

'Get some rest, Joyce,' Paula said. The woman nodded and left the room, and Glenross reached for Paula's hand.

'Come here,' he said. 'Thought you were Reggie. My sons

are very busy. It would be the same if I were dying. Sit down. Have they published my obit. yet?'

'No.'

'Good. Then I'm still here.' He grinned. 'Bastards,' he said.

'Don't talk.'

He reached over to the bedside table and pointed to the page proof. 'Look. Read that. "His biggest fight saving the takeover." Saving their skins they mean. Bastards. Think they've written me off.' He grabbed again at the page. 'Beaverbrook. Hated Beaverbrook. Alter that, will you. My Blitz headlines were better than his. Maybe it's because I'm a Londoner. That was a great page.' He struggled to sit up and Paula helped him with his pillow. 'That's it,' he wheezed. 'Life reduces one to finding a comfortable spot.'

She stroked his brow and whispered to him to try and sleep. He took her hand. 'I'd like to have slept with you,' he said, brightly. 'Always wanted to. Just wanted to say that.'

She smiled at him.

'You?' he asked. 'Sleep with someone?'

She nodded.

'Good. Enjoy it?'

'Yes.'

He smiled, closed his eyes and she sat in silence beside him looking at him. Gradually his breathing became heavier. Gently she tried to draw her hand away, but his grip tightened.

'Stay,' he whispered. 'You're the only one I can trust.'

# Seven

To the nurse tending the dying man, the three men in dark suits in the waiting-room seemed like vultures. For an hour they had been going over papers. Occasionally the tall one dictated into a small machine, while the little ferrety one argued with the third man. She heard the word 'contract' as she passed the door. You would think they could wait, she said to the Sister, instead of haggling over the old man's affairs just a few feet from his bed.

She passed again in front of the door and looked in. The oldest was doing the talking now.

'His mental, or indeed physical, condition may prevent such a contract or invalidate it if it is concluded,' he said.

She turned away, hoping that they might notice her disapproval, but they did not even acknowledge her. They were too busy.

'That's one for the consultant,' Schiff said. 'He's been very helpful.' He put a hand on the man's arm. 'Mr Chapel, Mr Bennet would like to retain your legal services on the *Register*, should . . .'

'As Lord Glenross's solicitor,' Chapel said, interrupting him, 'it would be quite improper of me to discuss that.'

'We're not asking you to discuss it,' Bennet said. 'We're asking you to be aware of it.'

Chapel shook his head. 'There isn't much time, Mr Bennet,' he said, got to his feet, excused himself and went into the ward.

Schiff watched him go, scowling at the man's back. 'He's

stalling,' he said. 'That bitch of a wife has queered it for us. She . . .'

Then he stopped as the nurse looked in.

'Telephone for you Mr Bennet. Paula Croxley.'

Schiff turned to Bennet and whispered, 'Don't take it. She may have changed her mind.' Then he turned back to the nurse. 'Mr Bennet's not available I'm afraid.'

'Or Lady Glenross, she said . . .'

'She asked not to be disturbed either. I'm sorry.'

She nodded and left. A moment later she came back and said that Lord Glenross would see them now. Bennet and Schiff got up fast and went past her into the room without a word. Chapel stood by the old man's bed with a contract. As they reached him, he handed it to Bennet. In silence he read through it, Glenross sipping water and watching him.

'I can't sign this,' Bennet said eventually.

'Why not?' Chapel asked.

'Once I agree to appoint her Editor, I can never fire her.'

'On the contrary,' Chapel said and pointed to a paragraph.

Bennet read: 'Appointment or removal of the Editor shall require the consent of a majority of national directors.'

Schiff looked up. 'Who are these schmucks?'

'These schmucks,' said Chapel, his voice curdled with distaste, 'are gentlemen of the highest probity.'

Schiff looked at the contract over Bennet's arm. 'Ormsby's down here,' he said.

'The national directors will guarantee the editorial freedom of the paper,' Chapel continued, talking to Bennet as if Schiff were not in the room.

'I'm prepared to guarantee that,' Bennet said.

Then Glenross cleared his throat and heaved himself into a sitting position. 'Mr Bennet,' he said. 'You are a shit. I recognise that because in, I hope, a rather more cultivated way, I am one too. It goes with the job perhaps. I have been driven reluctantly to the conclusion that the *Register*, in order to survive, needs a shit like you.'

Bennet took a step towards the bed and for a moment

Schiff thought he was going to strangle the old man. He reached out and pulled him back.

'But you're right,' Glenross continued. 'The paper also needs someone like Paula. And she will need protection.'

Schiff smiled at him. 'Can we consult?' Glenross nodded and he steered Bennet out, speaking softly, trying to calm him. 'Just give me time to redraft that paragraph and I'll shoot it full of loopholes.'

It was dark by the time they had worked out all the details. Bennet and Schiff were back at the old man's bedside, listening as Chapel read him Schiff's alterations.

' "If the Editor, on attested medical grounds, is considered mentally or physically incapable of holding the post, then he or she may be dismissed without reference to the board." ' He looked at Bennet. 'We have no objection.'

'Then I will sign,' said Bennet.

'The banker's order?' Chapel asked.

Schiff took a cheque from his pocket and held it up to the light so that Chapel could see it. Two and a half million dollars waiting for a signature. He handed it to Bennet who signed it without hesitation. Chapel took it and handed the contract to Schiff who passed it to the old man.

'Initial the alteration,' he said. No please, or would-you-mind, just a curt order, now that the cheque had been signed. Walter Schiff had never believed in cluttering up his sentences when there was business to be done.

Glenross hardly seemed to notice. He was staring at nothing. 'It's been in my family a hundred years,' he said.

Chapel held out a pen, but Glenross did not take it. Unexpectedly he began to laugh. 'Northcliffe wanted to buy us,' he said. 'Just before he went barmy. Nineteen twenty-two.'

A noise behind them made Bennet and Schiff turn. In the waiting-room they could see Clare and Ormsby pushing their way in and arguing with a nurse; they could hear her voice, patient, but firm, saying that she would not permit any more people at Lord Glenross's bedside. There was more than enough . . .

'Northcliffe was convinced,' the old man wheezed, 'that God was a homosexual.'

Bennet smiled and gestured towards the pen. Glenross took it and dropped it on the floor. Quickly, as if he were sprinting out of blocks, Schiff was on his knees scrabbling for it. Bennet turned and looked at the waiting-room. A doctor had arrived and the argument was getting heated, Clare pink-faced now.

'Rampaged through the hotel,' Glenross said. 'Stark naked, smashing all the mirrors. Didn't report *that* in his papers . . .' He laughed for a moment, then frowned as Schiff pressed the pen on him again, then he sighed and stabbed at the page, a fast scrawl and his signature glistened for a moment.

'Initial the alteration,' said Schiff.

Paula drove fast through the night, driving on autopilot, barely aware of the traffic or the lights or the junctions. Her mind was in confusion and she did not like herself very much. She had tried to rationalise away the previous evening. She had just been testing the idea of editing the paper on the old man, but he had seized on it, and, once he'd grasped the idea, he had been so enthusiastic. But still she felt guilty; her ambition had fought with her sense of decency and it had been no contest, and now she didn't know if she wanted the bloody job.

She glanced in the mirror. There was a smudge of dried jelly on her cheek from little Nicholas's kiss. She wiped it off. It had been the wrong thing to do, to go to her nephew's birthday party at a time like this, and she had got no sympathy from her sister. Kath had looked at her as if she despised her when she'd said that when Bennet had offered her the job she had actually forgotten about the baby. It can't be very important to you, Kath had said, then she'd added that she felt sorry for her. But Ian was coming back. He'd written. She wouldn't be a single parent. She could do both, couldn't she? Kath had shaken her head.

'You've only come to the party to observe the animals,' she'd said, 'to see if you wanted one.' And there was something in what she said.

Then Kath had handed Nicholas over to her and she had sung him to sleep, tucked him up and kissed him and, damn it, had begun to cry like some mumsy young girl . . . And then they wouldn't take her call and she'd stomped out and got into her car, her foot slipping on the clutch as she drove away and she'd seen the remains of a Marmite sandwich on her shoe . . .

A car hooted at her and she blinked away the trace of a tear, sniffed and concentrated on her driving. Five minutes later, she turned into the hospital car-park. At the main door she could see a scrum of reporters and two television crews. She got out and glanced at a spanking new Rolls-Royce parked nearby, and vaguely wondered who it belonged to, then she reached the group and recognised faces: old Archie from the *Register*, the lads from the *Mirror* and the *Mail*, and, in the middle, the smiling face of John Bennet, his voice breaking through the babble of questions and silencing them as they scribbled in notebooks and pushed out microphones.

'I have made firm guarantees of editorial freedom.'

'And who will be Editor?' someone asked.

'The best in Fleet Street.'

'Who's that?' A yell of interruption.

'. . . who will produce the best quality Sunday.' He smiled, said good-night and pushed through them, then saw Paula, reached for her arm and drew her towards the car-park. Now she knew who the Rolls belonged to. She could see Walter Schiff waiting beside it and a chauffeur in grey with a peaked hat. Behind, she heard the shouts, the competing questions: would the *Register* go down-market? What's your connection with Miss Croxley? Will you be pulling out of the *Mercury* bid?

66

'I have my car,' she said, but he was insistent, whispering to her, 'Forget that heap. No Editor of mine travels in a car like that.'

'I haven't accepted . . .'

'Get in,' he said.

She ducked in, blinking at the flash-guns, aware that she was on the wrong side of the ropes. She should be on the other side, asking the questions. She felt like the old saying: the poacher turned gamekeeper. Then the Rolls was gliding through the hospital gates.

'There are lots of things to talk about,' Bennet was saying. She looked at him, on her left, then at Walter Schiff, on her right. 'You can say anything in front of Walter,' he said. 'He's around almost as much as my shadow.'

She placed both hands on her stomach and gazed ahead. 'The baby,' she said.

'How many weeks is it?' Bennet asked.

'Three months.'

'No problem. Walter will fix it. Anything like that, see Walter.'

Fix it? she thought, then blinked as Schiff leant forward, opened the door of a cocktail cabinet built into the partition, drew out a bottle of champagne and thumbed it open.

Fix it? And now they were celebrating, handing her a glass, toasting each other, Bennet bright-eyed, as exuberant as a child.

'I thought I'd buy the Rolls as I'm now an essential part of Sunday,' he said.

The car rounded a corner and champagne frothed over the rim of her glass.

'The new *Register*,' said Schiff, and they echoed him in the toast. Paula raised her glass, then looked outside. A group of people on a corner was staring at them as if they were royalty. The others drank, but Paula did not join them. Fix it, she thought. It was hardly the time for celebration . . .

# Eight

The group of reporters outside the *Register* building was in a jovial mood. Door-stepping was normally boring, often uncomfortable and occasionally dangerous, but this was different. It was warm, the early morning sun had cleared St Paul's and from Mick's Café came the smell of coffee and cooking fat. None of them was far from base and so there would be no trouble getting the story back – and this was *their* story. They were all on their home patch, waiting to find out about one of their own, in their own trade – not waiting for some dozy rock star or nit-wit from showbusiness, or a politician with a sealed mouth. If this was a touch incestuous, no one minded, and it was only three hours till opening time.

The Street was quiet, most of the offices shut, and it was too early for the tourist buses. Then they stiffened as one, as the big Roller turned out of Chancery Lane towards them. It was shimmering in the sunlight. He was early, just like they'd been told – just like Rupert and Robert, up sharp to catch the unwary.

They clustered round the car as Bennet and Schiff got out, and hurled questions at them. Bennet stood on the steps of the building for a moment and smiled. 'You want a quote. I'll give you a quote. But first I would like to pay my respects to Charlie Glenross, who died yesterday.'

'You were with him just before . . . ?' someone asked.

'I was. Very shortly before. I knew him for only a short while but it was long enough to show me what a great man he was.'

68

'Why did he sell to you?' – from the *Mirror* man.

'We recognised each other as kindred spirits,' Bennet said. 'Those were his exact words.' He nodded solemnly, then smiled, lightening the mood. 'I'm going to point to those steps, OK?'

They moved forward. He pointed, then turned and smiled into the TV cameras. 'Saturday morning,' he said. 'Eight o'clock. Last Saturday, if a corpse was found on those steps, another paper would print the story first.' He paused. 'Not any more.'

Then he turned and ran up the steps, Schiff at his heels, the others following, murmuring among themselves.

An hour later Frank Ormsby took the lift to his office. He had arrived early so that he could have an hour or so to look round his office before the new broom swept him away. He stepped out of the lift and heard voices. The door was open. He could see Bennet, Schiff and a rather gorgeous young woman and a man in overalls clearing out his desk. He stopped, appalled, and listened.

'Miss Croxley's not at her sister's. Nor her flat,' said the young woman.

'Sod her,' Bennet said.

'Mr Greene wants to talk to you,' she added.

'Keep him out.'

'He wants to know who is editing the paper.'

'So do I, Debbie.' Ormsby watched Bennet glance at his watch. 'Smile at Greene,' he continued. 'Tell him to take the eleven o'clock. He's Deputy Editor for Christ's sake.' Then he shook his head. 'No. Tell him I'll see him at half-ten.' He snapped his fingers. 'Walter, find that stupid bitch.'

A movement to Bennet's left caught Ormsby's eye. The man in overalls was tugging at a locked drawer. This was too much for Ormsby. It was *his* drawer. There were personal effects in there.

'I have a key to that,' he said.

Bennet turned and smiled. 'Good morning, Frank,' he

said, as if it weren't Ormsby's office he was invading, as if he owned the damned place.

'I didn't expect you so early,' Ormsby said.

'People never do.'

Ormsby stepped in, handed the key to the removal man and collected a couple of framed photographs from the windowsill – his wife, and a family group, all smiling.

'You should have accepted the job when I offered it,' Bennet was saying. 'I never like this. Confrontation between people like you and me is a waste of scarce resources. I can offer you another job. I need someone of your calibre to run my Far East papers.'

Ormsby couldn't look at him. 'Thank you,' he said to the window. 'I have a job.'

'Already?'

'I'm a director of this newspaper. A national director.'

'Oh yes,' Bennet said. 'One of the men of probity who will safeguard the independence of this British institution.' Ormsby continued to stare through the window at nothing. Bennet was sneering at him now, at everything he held dear. 'Very important, Frank. But no financial power. That's not a job, Frank. It's a lunch club. The Far East job pays three hundred thousand dollars . . .'

Ormsby turned quickly and glared at him. 'This is still my paper. What right have you to walk in like this? Now she's got the paper for you, you're going to go back on your agreement, aren't you? You've never had any intention of making Paula Editor, have you?' He did not wait for a reply. Instead he answered himself. 'But you're going to. I'll see to that. And when you try and throw her out, you'll find out whether it's a lunch club or not.'

He turned and saw the man in overalls staring at him.

'Could you manage the rest please?' he asked him with a smile, then nodded at Glenross's portrait. 'I don't want the picture.' And he went out, for the last time.

For half an hour David Clare had sat motionless, staring at

70

the ceiling. He had phoned Ellie from home and told her not to come in till noon. There had been tears. She had cried, and it had taken him all his effort not to join her. He had come in the back way, avoiding the scrum at the main door. He had told the switchboard not to put through any calls. He had cleared out his desk drawers. It hadn't taken long. Now he sat quietly, thinking of the past, so that he wouldn't yet have to worry about the future.

A voice made him jump.

'Sorry.'

He looked up to see Paula at the door. She looked exhausted. Maybe, like him, she had had no sleep – victor and vanquished, united in exhaustion.

'Only lingering, Paula,' he said, smiled and shut an empty drawer. 'Bit like last day at school. I'm extraordinarily unmoved, you know. I suppose it hasn't hit me yet, but I'm quite looking forward to Saturday in the country.' He looked away from her at the walls, the framed first editions, of which he had been especially proud. 'It's a very English newspaper, you know. You can cut foreign coverage without a murmur, but try touching nature notes or the crossword and there'll be an outcry. You mustn't sneer at that.' He looked back at her. She was not sneering, just standing, looking around her. 'I shall miss the desk.' He stroked the leather top. 'Take care of it.' He pointed to an oil picture of a stern Edwardian. 'It was Bradwell's.'

Behind her he saw Schiff approaching. 'Ah, the bailiff,' he said and got to his feet, handed Paula the desk keys, wished her good luck and went out, ignoring Schiff, who, in turn, strode past him as if he were invisible.

'You haven't signed your contract,' he said to Paula.

She said nothing, followed Clare's example, ignored him and pushed past him, out into the corridor, heading for the lift.

Five floors above, Ted Lamb was trying to work the new man out. Bennet was in shirt-sleeves, tie loosened, going through a production schedule. The owner on his first day –

and demanding the impossible. Time, thought Lamb, to explain the facts of life.

'I can't guarantee there will be an issue tonight,' he said.

'Then there won't be one next week,' Bennet said.

'We've had threats before, Mr Bennet.'

'These aren't threats,' Bennet said, getting to his feet and looking down at him. 'They're promises.' He spoke quietly, gently, as if to a child who was complaining about going to bed too soon. 'The paper has one year to break even. One year to switch to the new technology. I'm not Glenross. I don't give a toss for old loyalties and high redundancies. Since Wapping, newspapers are a new ball game. Co-operate, or you're on the street, friend.'

Lamb didn't like what he heard. No one called Ted Lamb 'friend' – not in that tone.

'Are you going to break our agreements?' he asked.

There was a knock at the door. Bennet shouted, 'Wait', then turned back to Lamb.

'Agreements?' he said. 'They're a license to draw money for nothing. I know machine-rooms. I know all about double working, ghost working, regular casuals, casual casuals. From now on, comrade, you get paid for only one thing, and that's work. Otherwise I'll print and distribute it elsewhere. Your choice.'

Then he was at the door before Lamb could reply, jerking it open. Paula and Schiff walked in and Lamb walked out in silence, acknowledging no one, five feet six of hurt pride and ideas of mutiny.

Bennet slammed the door shut, took something from his pocket and lobbed it at Paula. She caught it and looked at it. It was a small piece of plastic.

'Your bleep,' Bennet said. 'I am one long piercing note. And where the hell have you been?'

'With Chapel,' she said.

'Why?'

'To see where I stand.'

Schiff picked up a file of papers from the desk. She saw her name on the cover. Her contract.

'You know where you stand,' Schiff said.

She smiled. 'I'm getting quite fond of Fred, you see,' and patted her stomach. 'Or Frederica. He's about two inches long. Weighs eighteen grams. Has ears – just about.'

Bennet sat at his desk and picked up a framed photograph of his son.

'What's to stop me having it and doing the job?' she said. 'We're talking about a weekly paper, not a daily. I'll have the child looked after. It won't interfere. You don't have to worry. While I'm having it . . .' she shrugged, 'I'll need a short time off, naturally, but I'll have a strong deputy.'

She looked away, biting her lip, fighting to keep the pleading tone at bay.

'You have five or six years,' Bennet said quietly. 'Dozens of chances to have another kid. One chance to be an editor. This one. If you want to take it, take it. You can't do both. If you want to be a mother, go ahead and be a mother. Make up your mind. We've a paper to get out.'

He was right and she knew it, but her trump card lay on his desk. A contract was a contract.

'You have to give me the job,' she said. 'It's in the contract of sale.'

Bennet looked at Schiff. 'Tell her,' he said.

'Sub-section 10B: appointment of Editor,' Schiff said in a high-speed monotone. 'Mental and physical health of same. Pregnancy would come under physical unsuitability for the post.'

'That's absurd,' she said, glaring from one to the other. 'That's discrimination.'

'We can block any case you bring for at least two years,' Schiff said. 'Probably three. Assuming you have the resources to bring one.'

'I'll see Chapel,' she said.

'Leave the bleep,' Bennet said.

She looked at it – an electronic umbilical cord to the proprietor. She smashed it on to the desk and walked out fast, her mouth set tightly shut, like a sprung trap, in case she said something she might regret, something unladylike.

The door slammed and Schiff grinned. 'Genius,' he said. 'That worked an absolute treat. You even had me believing you wanted her at one stage. It's a great deal. You get the paper without the liability. And Greene's perfect – a technician with no ideas of his own.'

Schiff danced a little jig, then stopped as he saw Bennet's face. The man should have been happy and triumphant, but he looked weary, like a fighter who knows he's just lost a round.

# Nine

The room was a mess: two walls of books, stacked haphazardly; mementoes from foreign trips competed for space: wooden carved figures, pieces of unglazed pottery, a Mayan drum. Her desk was an overflowing jumble of papers and books, the old typewriter half hidden, the title page of a manuscript limply curling from the carriage on *The New Wars* by Paula Croxley – just the title and the name, nothing more: six typed words illuminated by the last of the evening sun. She sat slumped in an armchair, scribbling a draft of a letter, then looked up and read aloud, 'Ormsby and Chapel will fight for me, but the problem is that he's in possession. Anyway I've plenty to do. There's the book and Fred or Frederica. I'm positive it was the day we went windsurfing and you had me al fresco . . .'

She threw the letter aside, ambled across the room, picked up the phone and dialled. It seemed to take forever. Finally an irritable voice came on the line. 'Operator,' Paula said, 'I booked a call to Beirut. I tried dialling but I can't get through.' She gave her name, said it was important, then hung up and went into the kitchen; better to tell him on the phone. Meanwhile she would get herself some supper and a glass of wine, or maybe a bottle . . .

An hour later, her doorphone squawked and brought her out of a half-sleep. Drowsily she reached for it. 'The bell sticks,' she said and yawned. 'Pull it out.' She jerked awake fully at the sound of a voice – the last person on earth she had expected.

Bennet came up fast, a bundle of newspapers under his arm. He walked in and looked around, frowning, as if this was somewhere he did not belong.

'This is where you live?' he said.

'It's a flat,' she said. 'I'm here – draw your own conclusions. What do you want?'

'I brought you tomorrow's paper.'

'I already have a paper boy.'

He ignored her and laid the paper on her desk, tried to spread it out, but the typewriter lay humped underneath. He grinned at her, beaming, his face flowing as if he were fuelled by electricity.

'My first off the press,' he said. 'Had to spread fifty-pound notes round the machine-room. All those bastards are interested in is money. Just wait till I'm dug in.' He pointed at the page. 'Look.'

She didn't – just stood by the door watching him. She could see her half-written letter beside him. She went over to it and covered it with a page of typescript. Bennet took no notice of her. He was turning the pages of the *Register*, tapping it with his right index finger. 'There's the Third World feature of yours hooked into the Sikh riots on the front. I wanted a good foreign story above the fold, but there's not enough impact.' He tapped another story. 'That was on television; should have been inside.' He pointed to the *Observer* lying on the floor. 'We missed that lead story.' Then he picked up *The Sunday Times*. 'This has more weight. Feel it. Who's going to buy the *Register*? I'm not talking about typefaces. Do you know what I'm talking about?'

She shrugged and began hunting round the room for matches.

'You should be out drinking with the boys,' she said. 'With the Editor.'

'There isn't one. Greene put it together but I've deferred the appointment till next week.'

She found the matches, lit her cigarette and watched as he strolled round the room, looking at it as if it were a zoo.

76

'Have you lived here long?'

'What do you want?' She was irritable. He'd had his say, now he could get the hell out. Soon she would have to tell him. He stood by the mantelpiece looking at a framed photograph. Paula and Ian on the beach, the windsurfing board at their feet.

'Is he the man?'

Her irritation bubbled over into anger. 'Will you tell me what you want?'

He turned and looked down at her. 'I never had any intention of giving you the job,' he said.

For a moment she thought she was going to hit him, but it passed. She had lashed out three times in her life – each time she hadn't thought about it. She'd just done it instinctively. Instead, she turned her back on him and said softly, 'Will you please get out of my flat.'

'It was a ludicrous thought,' he said.

'Thanks.'

'You thought so too,' he said. 'It took me all my time to sell the idea to you. But I think I've made a mistake, or nearly made a mistake. With all this concentration on new presses, colour, computers, there's one thing people are forgetting.'

Reluctantly, her curiosity overcoming her anger, she turned and looked at him. He was wiping newsprint off his hands with a tissue. 'The editorial. You know, the stuff that people actually read. Fleet Street is full of bad editors. Organ-grinder's monkeys.'

He looked back at the photograph. Paula in her bikini. He seemed, to her, to be leering at it.

'I don't like you,' he continued. 'I don't like your politics, your feminism, the way you dress. And I detest people who smoke. But you can write and smell out a story and stick to your guns, which could be a pain in the ass for me, but if it brings in readers, I can always take aspirin.'

He turned and looked at her. 'You see, in selling the idea to you, I sold it to myself. It might still be ludicrous, but it might work and, if it does, my God what a trick!'

She reached for the photograph and laid it face down. 'What am I supposed to do?' she said. 'Fall down on my knees in gratitude? Ludicrous. You will make me into an editor. You make me sound like Eliza.'

He frowned.

'Doolittle,' she explained. 'Pygmalion. Bernard Shaw.'

'I don't read fiction,' he said.

She smiled at him. He had had his say. Now it was her turn. Then he could get out.

'I don't like *you* very much,' she said. 'You're ignorant. Sexist. That creep you always have with you, where is he? Somewhere in the woodwork? I've had the chance to read some of your American papers, by the way.' She went to her desk. Behind it was a pile of newspapers. She scrabbled through, came up with the *Cincinnati Banner* and waved it in front of his face: a picture of a gruesome murder on the front page and a seventy-point headline screeching *City In Terror*. 'Social concern?' she said. 'This semi-literate muck?'

He snatched it from her, angrily crumpled it and threw it away, and now it was her turn to think that she might be hit. Briefly he looked murderous and she'd seen murderers. She stepped back, then he passed his hand over his face and picked up the *Register*, caressing it, folding it gently and smoothing out the creases. 'That muck,' he said, pointing to the crumpled paper on the floor, 'bought the *Register*.'

'Why?'

He did not answer. Instead he looked at her, head cocked on one side like a curious puppy. 'What's your background?' he asked.

'Father's a doctor. Mother is, or rather was, a radiologist. Middle-class boring. Why do you ask?'

'Mine wasn't boring,' he said. 'Poor, but not boring. I've worked harder and taken more risks than you will in two lifetimes. In the last ten years I've made more money than most millionaires. Sure, I'm ignorant.' And the anger flared again. 'Do you think I don't care what people say about me?' She shrugged and reached for the packet of cigarettes. 'I want to produce a great newspaper and I can't do it in the States. People see me as they think I am.'

She put another cigarette in her mouth and reached for matches.

'Don't smoke, please,' he snapped and snatched the packet from her, then fluttered his hands and apologised, handed them back and struck a match for her, the anger gone from him now. He held up his hands as if in surrender. 'Look, I'm sorry, but I'm not accustomed to being with people I respect. I'm sorry about bursting in, saying those things.' He picked up the *Register* and handed it to her. 'Look at it, Paula, then look at the opposition. Greene will produce a competent paper, but a merely competent paper will go down. I know what's right when I see it, but I can't do it. You can. Together we can.'

She shook her head and sat at her desk, two fingers of her left hand gently massaging the pulse in her temple. He knelt next to her and took her hand. 'Is it the baby,' he asked gently, 'or the relationship?'

'Both,' she said, then looked at him. 'I could do both.'

'No.'

'Then I don't do it.'

He paused for a moment, then spoke slowly and quietly. 'That first year is make or break. You know that it's impossible for you to do both. Just give me that first year, then have a baby.' She had put the photograph on the desk and he nodded at it. 'Does he know about it yet?'

She did not answer. He knew from her expression. She closed her eyes, took a deep breath, then looked at him. 'It will be just the same in a year's time,' she said.

'No.'

'It will. We'll be having exactly the same arguments . . .'

The phone rang and she twitched, then he was on his feet and heading for the door. 'I promise,' he said.

'You promise? How can I believe a word you say?' The phone continued to ring, jangling her nerves. 'Please go away.'

He went to the door and she ran after him, shouting, 'There are plenty of others. Why me? Will you please go?'

He nodded and went out. She slammed the door and stood for a moment leaning against it. The phone rang and rang. In her imagination it was like the old cartoons, the receiver bouncing on the cradle. Next to it, Ian smiled at her out of the frame, his arm around her naked waist. She took a step towards it, then leant back again against the door, closed her eyes and kept them closed until there was silence once more.

# Ten

Walter Schiff had been as good as Bennet's word. He had fixed it OK. A day and a night in the clinic and Fred was gone. It *was* Fred, not Frederica. She had asked. Now he was gone and all that remained was a residue of guilt. She had known she would feel guilty. She had written a series on depression years ago and had interviewed women who had had abortions. When she had written the piece, she had tried to skate round the clichés, remembering Cudlipp's famous memo: avoid clichés like the plague. But now, two days after, she was living another cliché: hard work was the antidote to depression. She had scrubbed away the tears and made up her mind to forget Fred and get on with being Paula Croxley, Editor.

The brand new D-registration black Bentley sat gleaming at the kerb, attracting admiring glances. She had got rid of Bennet's flowers at the clinic but she could not send back the car at the door.

It was a warm morning. Brook Green was lush. The postman grinned at her and whistled at the sight of the car. She smiled at him and slipped inside, closing the door gently behind her. The delivery driver had given her an envelope with the keys. She opened it and drew out a cassette. It was printed *Register: Week One.*

She slipped it into the stereo deck and switched on.

'Like it, Eliza?' Bennet's voice boomed at her in stereo.

She turned it down and sat back. 'Had to go to the States,' he said, cheerfully. 'Back Saturday. All my papers have fifty-week assessment periods. This is week one. By week fifty, the *Register* will break even and you will be a household name.'

She hit the *off* button and leant her head on the dashboard. 'Jesus Christ,' she whispered. 'What have I done?'

By the time she reached Fleet Street, she knew exactly what she had done and what she was expected to do. Bennet's voice had bludgeoned her eardrums all the way in. There were too many sections in the paper, he said. Perhaps we should go back to three or even two. The back bench cover their asses too much. They need a female boot to shake them up. He wanted her to put her feminism on ice for a year. 'Take it from an old sexist,' he boomed. 'Flash your eyes at the printers and we might manage an extra edition.'

He had fired the Advertising Manager and hired someone called Tim Moodie, a man, he said, who would sell his grandmother for an eight-column ad.

The lights at Chancery Lane were red. She tapped her fingers on the dashboard and listened for the second time to Bennet's final suggestion.

'Your first issue will climax at a supper party at the Savoy. I want every jaw to drop when you walk in. Get that Women's Page Editor off her elegant ass. Why not use yourself in a special feature: *Power Dressing For Women.*'

'Crap,' she said as the lights changed. Power dressing. But even as she swore, she knew she would do it, however reluctantly. She owed it to Fred to succeed, and, besides, she knew quite well that a small part of her would not object to becoming a household name.

From the beginning there were problems. She had anticipated trouble and there was trouble. She knew that there would be envy and back-stabbing and innuendo, and, in her first two days, she encountered a surfeit of all of them. The new man, Moodie, was large and florid and tried to bully her, wanted page three for himself, an ad. instead of editorial. Toby Greene had cleared it, he said. Paula nodded. If there was going to be a battle, then it was better sooner than later.

82

She went hunting for Greene and found him in the newsroom talking to Jim Fowler and a young reporter she barely knew, who had joined the paper while she was away. All she knew about him was that his name was David Stone and that he was regarded as potentially good, but he still had the arrogance of someone yet to make his name. As she approached, she caught the tail end of the conversation, Greene telling Stone to drop the investigation. Stone looked sullen and mutinous and turned away as she reached them, mumbling a hello at her, then he shambled off towards the library.

'Drop what?' she asked.

'Spy scandal of the century,' said Greene.

'Shock horror,' Fowler added, then saw the anger in Paula's face. 'Am I wanted?' he asked. He wasn't. He left them to it, wondering what was going on.

'Page three,' she said to Greene.

'Are you volunteering?'

'What?'

'To pose.'

It wasn't funny. She did not smile. 'I'm getting very bored with being looked at as a novelty pair of tits,' she said. 'Did you clear that ad. on page three with Moodie?'

'Yes.'

'Why didn't you refer it to me?'

'Because I referred it to Bennet,' he said, smiling, acting calm in the face of her anger.

'When?'

'Before he left.' He held up his hands, palms towards her. 'Sorry. I understood that was my area.'

'Did you? Well, I think we'd better define our areas.'

'Bennet's done that.'

She nodded and looked round the room, at reporters and sub-editors, working, pretending not to notice them.

'What did he say to you, exactly?' she asked.

'I run the paper. You provide the creative flair.'

'I don't know what that means,' she said.

He smiled, pink-cheeked and confident. 'Neither do I, love,' he said.

Love. The smug, patronising bastard, she thought. She moved a step closer. '*I'm* the Editor, love,' she said.

'That's your title.'

She had had enough. 'Why don't you go, Toby?' she said softly.

'Are you firing me?'

'I'm suggesting you look for another job.'

'Have you suggested this to Bennet?'

'I make the editorial appointments.'

He turned away and gazed across the newsroom. When he looked back at her, he was still smiling – the smile, Paula thought, that one day would get him a knee in the groin.

'I'll tell you why I'm not going Paula,' he said. 'Because you have my job. Because you can't do it. You won't survive. On Saturday night you'll realise that. When the lawyer flaps and you have to pull a story, and they tell you if you do you'll miss the trains to Scotland, and you don't know whether to believe them or not, you'll realise that. Getting the paper out needs work and experience, not creative flair. You're the front dressing, love, don't you realise that?'

She was about to answer, when they were interrupted by a small man striding towards them, whistling tunelessly and carrying a sheaf of papers: the week's production schedule. He smiled at Paula and handed the schedule to Greene.

'How's that, Toby?' he asked.

Greene flipped through the pages. 'Pix for inside home pages by half-seven.' He looked at the man. 'Can't you clear all the pictures for the centre and the weekend section on Friday?'

'If we get them.'

It was as if Paula was invisible, or as if she were a secretary or a messenger, someone who wouldn't have anything to do with the schedule. They were ignoring her, as if she was too unimportant to understand. She turned and walked away. Another time. There would be other times for battle; not now.

As she passed Stone's desk, she saw a thick envelope by the phone. Stone was out, his jacket draped over the back of the chair: the old ploy – probably across at the Harrow, nursing his grievance. She picked up the file and tucked it under her arm. Later, when she had a few spare minutes, maybe she would take a look at it. It was a story. She understood stories. Maybe not the intricacies of a schedule; too dumb for that, but not too dumb to understand the basics . . .

The last of the evening sunshine, slicing through the venetian blinds, made a zebra pattern on Paula's desk. She had left the cuttings to one side, the top one from the *Guardian* showing a Cruise missile and the headline: *American Concern Over Defence Leaks*. She was gazing at a seven by five black-and-white print of a grey-haired man in his mid-forties, an arrogant, patrician face, the caption pasted onto the bottom right: *Robert Stead, Assistant Secretary at the Ministry of Defence, found dead at his home of a heart attack*. It was dated a month earlier.

She pulled a tape from the package, inserted it into her recorder and recognised Stone's voice.

'What's your name?'

'David Bowie.' The voice was shrill, the telephone line bad.

'If you won't tell me your . . .'

'I can't,' the voice screamed. 'I can't. The Russians killed him.'

'Why?'

'For the papers.'

'What papers?'

'It's my fault. It's . . .'

Paula clicked the machine off and yawned, suddenly feeling a pang of loneliness. There was no one she could talk to now. Kath disapproved of her. Ian would be angry if he found out about the abortion, and, besides, there was no longer any sign of him coming back. The others would treat her differently, now that she was no longer one of them. Then she swore at herself. This was no time for self-pity. She had made her decision and she would simply have to make the best of it.

There was a knock on the door and Alan Merton looked in. 'Just wondered if you'd like a drink,' he said.

She smiled. 'Bless you Alan,' she said. A friendly face, a man with not a hint of deviousness in him. Just at that moment Alan Merton's was the kind of face she needed. On the way out she asked him about Stead.

'Heart attack,' he said. 'David Stone's been trying to make something of it. Keeps pointing out that the inquest was adjourned and that there was a wound on the temple, probably caused by bashing his head on the coffee-table. His keys were found a couple of streets away. He was supposed to fly to Brussels for a NATO meeting on the night he died. No one knows why he came back.'

'Maybe he just fell ill,' Paula said.

'Maybe.'

'There's nothing very hard in the file.'

'I know,' Merton said, nodding agreement. 'And deep throat sounds like a crank.'

'And Stone? Is he good?'

'He did a good story on bent coppers when he was on the *Birmingham Mail*. He's bright. He gets people's backs up because he won't do run-of-the-mill stuff.'

'Determined to find another Philby? Whether there is one or not?'

Merton nodded. 'Yep, that's about it.'

They had reached the street now, through the side entrance into an alley off Fleet Street. Paula turned left and Merton stopped.

'I thought we'd use the Crown,' he said.

She stopped and turned. 'They'll all be at the Feathers.'

Merton looked at his shoes and Paula suddenly understood. 'I see,' she said. 'It's character assassination time, is it? Mine.'

Merton shrugged and looked up. 'Clare never went there.'

'I'm not Clare.'

86

But still Merton did not move.

'What is it?' Paula asked.

'There's a lot of feeling . . .'

'I did the dirty on Clare.'

'Well you did, didn't you?'

'So did Greene,' she said angrily. 'He's one of you, I suppose. Do you think Clare was worth saving?'

He said nothing. She turned away and again he stopped her. 'Paula. Have you seen the *Eye*?'

'No.'

'Nobody's told you?' He looked shocked, incredulous as he drew the magazine from his inside pocket. On the cover was a photograph of Paula and Bennet, laughing together and he was saying: '*Why stop at putting the paper to bed?*'

She snatched it from him and turned to the inside page, the Street of Shame column, her lips moving as she read the piece; for once they'd got it right. Bennet had offered her the job at night in her flat. There was no need for nods, winks or innuendo, just the plain facts were enough: but how did they know? Only she knew and Bennet and probably Walter Schiff, and now everyone knew.

'You don't believe this rubbish, do you?' she said to Merton.

'No.'

Then she turned and headed down the alley towards the pub, almost at a run, thinking of the things she would do to Bennet when he came back, thinking that life was easier in Beirut. At least in Beirut the bullets came at you from the front.

She strode in and saw them all clustered round the bar, heard the laughter, the glutinous voice of Sutcliffe: '. . . a toast to the mole, whoever he may be. To the scourge of Paula Knickersinatwist . . .' the last syllable exploding in the sudden silence, as she came towards them, Merton a pace behind. *Private Eye* lay on the bar, damp with beer.

'Lager,' she said to Len, the barman. 'And a pint of Special, please.'

She picked up the magazine and looked at Sutcliffe. 'I hope no one thinks there's any truth in this,' she said.

Silence. She looked from one to the other. No one met her gaze until she got to Greene, who smiled. 'Of course not,' he said. Everyone laughed as if Greene was top of the bill at the Palladium, the gusts of laughter blowing away the tension.

'I'm buying,' Paula said, but suddenly no one was thirsty. Greene said he was all right thanks. Fowler said that the train to Orpington called him, and again there was a silence, broken by the scraping of a chair. She turned to see David Stone getting up and holding out an empty glass.

'I'd like a vodka and lime please,' he said.

She nodded briefly, then turned back to Greene.

'Page three will be editorial, Toby.'

'Can we discuss that later?' he said.

'There's nothing to discuss. Page three will be home news.'

She handed Merton his beer. Len offered change. She took it and dropped a couple of coins. Stone was first to bend and pick them up. He handed the money to her, but got no thanks.

'I can't see anything in your story,' she said.

'So I don't get my drink?'

Her anger evaporated. She apologised and ordered it. When she turned back to him, she was calm, in control once more. 'I'm afraid I agree with Toby,' she said. 'Your mystery caller. He's a nutter.'

'Probably.'

She looked at him. His arrogance had been replaced by an air of defeat. This was a sensitive young man, she thought, a man of peaks and troughs of emotion and an ulcer by thirty-five. What he needed was someone to show an interest.

'Was Stead married?' she asked.

He nodded. 'Two children.'

'Have you talked to his wife?'

'She's hiding somewhere. The house is shut up.'

88

'OK, so, the next time your nutter phones, say the police are getting close.'

'But they're not.'

'He doesn't know that. If he's a hoaxer, you've lost nothing. If he's genuine, and thinks he's about to be picked up, he might talk to you first.'

He smiled and nodded, gulped his drink and went out fast. She'd thrown him a bone and he was chasing it – another one on her side. Merton and Stone, her allies, but it was a terribly small army in a place like Fleet Street.

Saturday night should have been the most exciting night of her life. Everyone was in the machine-room waiting for the big press to roll and produce her first paper. Bennet looked incongruous in his dinner-jacket among the sweats in their greasy overalls. The whole back bench was clustered round the machinery. Greene had a proof in his hand and looked happy. She glanced at him, then looked away. He had won. Page three was a bloody advert. She should have been happy, but instead she was depressed. The paper was not good enough and she knew it only too well.

Greene came across and leant against a steel casing. 'I'm firing Stone,' he said. 'OK?'

'Why?'

'He just buggered off.'

'Where?'

'No idea. No message. He's had the statutory written warning.'

She was about to answer when she heard Ted Lamb shouting at her, 'Paula, Paula, it's all yours.' Then a photographer was adjusting his lens and Bennet was smiling and beckoning her.

'OK?' Greene persisted.

'Do what you like,' she said, then Bennet was at her side, smiling, taking her arm, leading her to the old Goss rotary. Cameras flashed. She should have felt like royalty launching a ship, but she only felt silly. However, she smiled as she pressed the *on* switch. It grumbled into life and the paper began to run through; loud cheers, Bennet still smiling. Moments later Ted Lamb handed her a copy of the paper, grinning at her like a midwife tenderly handing over a baby, and Bennet had his arm around her, asking how she felt about it, and wasn't it a good front page?

'We should have led on India,' she said.

'No no,' he said. 'Too much on television. You were absolutely right to go for the strike. More of our own stuff. Strong pic.'

He moved even closer, hugging her to the dinner-jacket. She smelled aftershave.

'Proud?' he asked.

'Yes, of course.'

Then the camera flashed again and she remembered what he had done and she broke away from him. 'I want to see you,' she said.

'After the Savoy. What a line-up I've got for you. One Minister. The American Ambassador.' He checked his watch. 'You'd better change.'

But she was not interested in parties, at the Savoy or anywhere else.

'Are you going to bring an action?' she asked.

'What?'

'Against *Private Eye*?'

He leant closer, his smile a grimace. 'Not here, Paula.' But she was not to be warned off.

'If you don't, I will.'

People were turning, trying to hear what was being said. They were centre stage and Bennet's smile was beginning to fray at the edges.

'Are you crazy?' he said. 'That publicity is worth fifty thousand copies.'

'Is that what you told them?'

He reared back, astonished, as if she had thrown a punch at his face. '*I* told them,' he said, and laughed as if it were the

90

craziest idea he'd ever heard. She scowled at him, then turned and pushed her way through the throng, vaguely aware of their curious faces. A lovers' tiff – that's what they would be thinking.

Ten minutes later she was sitting in the pub with Alan Merton. The first editions of the quality Sundays were scattered on the table and Merton was looking for the right thing to say.

'You can't expect to do anything in a week.'

But she wouldn't be consoled. 'I feel humiliated,' she said. 'I feel thick. Stupid. The ad's on page three.'

'You chose the wrong ground to fight on,' he persisted. 'The business side.'

'And the *Eye* story . . .'

'Go to the Savoy,' he said.

She looked hard at him, anger building again. 'And be what they want me to be, front dressing?'

'Yes.'

'A publicity stunt?' she said, her voice rising almost to a yell. 'His woman?'

Merton placed both hands on her shoulders. He had been around a long time. He was the sensible one, every young reporter's friendly uncle, the man who always made sense.

'Paula, he wants to create this picture of a powerful woman Editor. Why don't . . .'

'Woman, yes,' she interrupted. 'Powerful, no.'

'Powerful, yes,' he argued. 'See, he won't be able to stop the process. The more he builds you up into a public figure, the more you'll be in a position to fight.'

She nodded. He was right. He was making sense again. Then she looked at the paper crumpled on the table, the sports pages sodden with lager.

'Fight for what, Alan?' she asked.

He was about to answer, when the table was bumped by someone squeezing past. They looked up to see Stone. He was tense, oozing repressed excitement.

'Where the hell have you been?' Merton asked.

'To see my mystery caller.'

Paula gestured him to sit down. 'What happened?' she asked.

'He didn't turn up.'

'Why didn't you ask me?' Merton said.

Stone shrugged. 'Jim was on the desk when he called. I'm sorry.' He reached into his jacket and pulled out a cellophane package. 'But when I got back, this had come. By hand.' Paula reached for it. 'Don't take it out,' he said sharply. 'Please give me a moment.' She nodded and he continued: 'On the night he died, Stead was due to fly to Brussels. He'd checked in. His ticket and boarding pass were found in his pocket.' He held up the package. 'Look,' he said and his hand was trembling.

They peered through the cellophane at a Sabena ticket. It was an open return, the forward flight missing, and a boarding pass.

'The name on it is Michael Neilson.'

'He was travelling with Stead?' Paula asked. 'Your nutter?'

Stone nodded, excitement flowing from him like electricity. 'I've checked with Sabena. They were both called repeatedly. The plane left late.' He looked at her and blushed. 'If you hadn't believed me . . .'

'I wouldn't go so far as . . .'

'I told him the police were getting close,' he said, speaking fast, stumbling over the words. 'He's hooked.'

Paula shushed him. 'Take it easy. You were fired an hour ago.'

The colour left his face. He swallowed, looked as if he was going to vomit, then Paula smiled. 'For God's sake don't go off without telling people where you are.'

He nodded and sat back, shivering slightly, and then got up and went to the bar. He needed a stiff one, or maybe three.

Paula stared for a moment at the cellophane package, then looked at Merton. 'Funny how easy it is to forget why we do this job,' she said, and Merton smiled along with her. She looked out into the street, then down again at the paper, opened it to the features pages, stared at herself in the black evening suit. Power dressing. She looked good in black. The hell with it. The suit was still hanging in the Women's Page room upstairs. She'd wear it to the Savoy. It would be a nice touch.

# Part Two

# Eleven

In the six months since the new Editor had taken over, David Stone had waited expectantly for something to happen. At one point he thought he could make it happen alone, but his one big story had dried up on him. His contact had vanished. It was a dead-end – and other things had come to nothing, no matter how hard he tried. But the difference with Paula, compared to the dreadful old man Clare, was that there was a chance for him. She was a reporter's Editor. She had done it all. She knew the problems. So many editors had come up through the production side, never been out in the cold, wouldn't know a story if it came up and belted them in their expense-account paunches. But Paula was different and soon things would change, as soon as the new investigative unit was formed. He could work for Paula Croxley and once he was doing a proper job, he reckoned he would just about work for her for nothing.

He had set the alarm to watch breakfast television and he lay back in bed, watching his Editor smile at him in colour, seated on a burgundy leather sofa, fielding questions from an interviewer. She looked relaxed, a natural, perfectly at ease.

'And how would you regard John Bennet now, Paula?'

'He's the most remarkable man in Fleet Street.' She shrugged. 'What else do you expect me to say?'

The interviewer laughed. 'And how closely do you work together?'

'Not as closely as that.'

Stone grinned and slipped out of bed. Smart woman. Over

the past six months she had turned all the gossip to her advantage. Even the bitchiest in Fleet Street had been forced to admit it. It was hard to snipe at someone who invited the fire, then returned it tenfold.

'You have said that you plan to carry out major investigations?' the interviewer was asking.

'Yes. We're getting a team together right now.'

Stone whooped and snapped his fingers. 'You tell them, Ed.,' he said. That was David Stone she was talking about, part of the new team. He could not wait to get started.

Two hours later he was at his desk, drinking lukewarm coffee and reading the papers. He looked up as Jim Fowler came over. You could always tell when Fowler was approaching. He wore nylon shirts and, even upwind of him, even before the pubs opened, it was not difficult to sense that the Deputy News Editor was on the prowl.

'Morning David,' he said. 'How's the special investigation unit?'

'Thin on the ground.'

Fowler slapped a scientific report on his desk. It looked like *War and Peace*; it could have choked a horse, Stone reckoned.

'Ted's in Moscow,' Fowler said. 'So how about four hundred words on food from microbes?'

Stone groaned. 'Since I'm coming under Features, I could tell you to piss off.'

'*When* you come under Features,' Fowler said. '*When* the money comes through for your little empire. Until then . . .' He slapped the report on the desk, causing papers to flutter and the coffee to ripple under newly formed skin. Stone watched him go, then looked up to see Merton frantically waving him over, the phone at his ear. He moved fast and skidded up to Merton's desk.

'It's Neilson,' Merton said, hand over the receiver. 'I want to record him. I'll put him through to Paula's office.'

Stone felt a sudden rush of excitement, followed by panic. 'We'll lose him,' he said.

'Just keep him going.' He handed over the phone and ran.

'Hello, Mike,' Stone said, fighting to sound calm. 'I was wondering what happened to you . . . You went away? Where? It's been ages . . . Listen, I want to transfer you so we can talk in private. Can I have your number? I won't tell the police, that's up to you . . . Well, just hang on – there'll be the odd funny noise. Hang on.' He dropped the phone, turned and ran through the newsroom, bumped into Greene, apologised and careered into a desk.

'What's with Steve Ovett?' Greene asked, watching him rush towards the Editor's office.

'I wish he was as fast with his copy,' Fowler said, and the two men smiled at one another, enjoying their little joke.

Stone careered into Paula's office. She was standing beside her desk, Merton next to her. He glanced at the amplified phone with the rubber recorder attached and clenched his fists.

'Got him?'

Merton shook his head.

'Bloody switchboard,' Stone raged. 'They haven't lost him, have they?'

'Calm down,' Merton said softly.

'Did you take his number?' Paula asked, and the voice of the operator answered, crackling through the room. 'He won't give it.'

Merton looked at Stone. 'He's in a pay-box.'

Stone swore, closed his eyes, listened to the squeals from the phone, then the operator saying she was putting him through. Stone leant into the amplifier. 'Mike?' he said, almost pleading.

'I've only got one more 10p,' The voice trembled and Stone crossed his fingers.

'You can trust me, Mike. Give me your number.'

'They're going to put it on me.'

'Mike . . .'

'I wouldn't,' the voice said. 'No way would I. We were going to Brussels together. We quarrelled and he went home and I . . .'

99

'Mike, I can't do anything unless I meet you.'

'I didn't kill him, I didn't.'

'Then you've nothing to be frightened of.'

'I don't want the police . . .'

Stone cursed as he heard the pips bleep at them.

'Give us your number,' he yelled.

No reply, just the sound of a coin going into the slot, dropping through, the pips continuing. 'Bloody hellfire,' Stone grunted, then Neilson was back on the line and whining, 'I need help.'

Paula reached out, put her finger against Stone's lips and moved forward. 'Mike,' she said.

'Who's that?'

'I'm the Editor. Paula.'

There was a moment's silence, then: 'I saw you. On telly. I need help. I need money.'

'We can't help you if we don't meet you.'

'You'll tell the police.'

'I think you should go to the police, but that's up to you.' Stone looked at her. She was terrific – not a trace of tension, like some goddam Samaritan talking to a suicide attempt. 'Will you come here?' she asked.

'No!' It was a scream, and made Stone and Merton jump. But Paula was unmoved.

'Then David will come to you,' she said. 'All right?'

Silence.

'Mike?'

'All right.' A quiet agreement followed by the beeping of the pips.

'Where?' she said urgently.

'See Andy. Piccadilly Tube. Saxa . . .' And he was cut off. She looked up. 'Saxa?'

'Saxophone,' Merton said.


Fifteen minutes later Stone and Merton were roaming the Piccadilly Circus tube looking for a saxophone player. It should have been easy, but Stone knew the problems. The

100

kids kept getting moved on and fined. Busking was illegal and buskers were hardly the most reliable types to find. They had sent Morris, the photographer, to lie in wait at the hotel in Bayswater, then they had tried each of the five entrance corridors and the Piccadilly line and finally they found him, at the bottom of the escalators on the Bakerloo line. He was a ragged young man with a sad face.

'Andy?' said Stone, and dropped two pound coins in his case.

The young man stopped playing and looked at him.

'Very nice,' Stone said.

'That's for the old ladies. I save the real stuff for the rush-hour punters.'

Merton pushed forward. '*Sunday Register*,' he said. 'We're meeting Mike. This is David Stone.'

'He said one person.'

'I'm the News Editor.'

'Big stuff,' he said sarcastically. 'Can I see your Press card?'

Merton showed him.

'Where is he?' Stone said, getting impatient now.

'Inflation's worse this month.'

Another couple of coins tinkled into his case. 'Thanks,' he said and nodded to the escalator. 'Up there. He's been watching you.'

They turned, and saw a pale young man standing at the top of the escalator. He was thin, maybe in his mid-twenties, wearing a leather jacket and patched jeans. Stone was first to move, running up the escalator, pushing past people standing in groups. Fuckin' tourists, he thought as he struggled past. As he reached the top, he swore again, aloud this time. Neilson had gone. Then he saw him – leaning against a wall. Stone walked slowly up to him. The young man looked scared and exhausted.

'Hello, Mike,' he said . . .

In the cab they were silent, Neilson nervous, biting his fingernails, staring out. All he wanted to know was where they were going. Stone told him. An anonymous hotel in Bayswater, as safe, he said, as houses, but Neilson did not laugh. The cab gurgled to a halt and Merton was out first, paying off the cab while Stone helped Neilson out and looked around. Across the street he could see Jim Morris's car, the lens poking through the window. Stone steered Neilson away from the cab, waited a moment to let Morris get his snaps, then the three men hurried up the steps.

The hotel was a quiet place. They said nothing while at reception, in the lift or walking along the corridor – not until Merton had the key in the lock of Room 310.

'Who's in there?' Neilson wanted to know.

'No one's in there, Mike,' Stone said. 'You saw us book it.'

Merton turned the key, then was pushed to one side as Neilson kicked the door open and looked in. It was a standard room – a single bed, a lamp and a television set, net curtains gently fluttering at the open window. Neilson stepped in as if he were entering a minefield, looked around and went into the bathroom. Merton and Stone came in, shut the door and Merton went to the phone.

'South Sea magic bubbles,' Neilson said, coming back into the room, holding a plastic sachet in his left hand, then stopped as he saw Merton by the phone.

'What are you doing?'

'Room service,' Merton said.

'What for?'

'Coffee.'

'I'll order the coffee.' The voice was shrill again and insistent. 'Put it down.' Merton hesitated for a moment. There was a stand-off, then Neilson dropped the sachet, dipped into his pocket and flipped out a knife. The blade sprang from the hilt with a sharp click. Merton put the phone down.

'Give me the key,' Neilson shouted.

Merton stepped forward.

'Throw it.'

Merton tossed it at him. Neilson caught it with his free hand and turned towards Stone, menacing, the knife held throat-high. Stone shook his head and flopped on the bed, like a dog offering its throat in defeat. This was going to be one bitch of a day, he thought.

Walter Schiff had always prided himself on his ability to thrive on problems and so now, logically, he should be in prime condition because there was a mountain of problems, at home and abroad. He swigged coffee and looked down at Park Lane. He could see the Rolls at the kerb. Bennet would be waiting for him. He gathered up his papers, slid them into his briefcase and went out, thinking hard, making a list of the problems to be solved, in order of priority. The big one was the printers' strike in New York. The *Courier* took precedence. In London the machine had broken down again. They had lost two hours on Saturday night which meant no Scottish edition.

On the way down, he glanced again at his copy of the *Register*. A double column box on the front proclaimed: *The New Register — More Readers, More Pages, More Advertisers*. And more fuckin' problems, he muttered to himself. Costs were up and that bloody Croxley woman was badgering Bennet for a budget for some goddamned investigative unit or something, and, what was worse, Bennet was actually considering giving it to her. It was his one weakness. It was history repeating itself. Watching her on TV that morning, Bennet had seemed entranced by her. Called her a natural performer. Yeah, Schiff had thought. Performing what? But he had kept quiet. Then there was the proposed deal with Forest to print the *Mercury*. Bennet wanted to invest two million in a new machine-shop, which meant that the Forest deal had to go through. But as far as Walter Schiff was concerned, the man was making another mistake.

Bennet was sitting, pale-faced and impatient, in the back of the Rolls and looked up angrily as Schiff ducked into the car and shook his head.

103

'They swore the print contract would be here before I left,' Bennet said.

'Technicalities,' Schiff said.

'Are you sure?'

'We've had industrial snoops on the Deputy Chairman of Forest . . .' He snapped his fingers, trying to remember the name. Bennet supplied it. 'Turner.'

'Yeah, Turner. We know how many calories he has for breakfast. It looks like a clean deal. Moodie can sign it.'

Bennet shook his head and gestured to the chauffeur to start the car, then picked up the print-outs. 'I've just had another look at the figures,' he said. 'I don't like leaving London without that print contract.'

Schiff shrugged. What was there to say? They had to get to New York to sort out the strike. The print contract could wait. They sat in silence through Chiswick and over the elevated section, then, on the motorway, Bennet grunted an oath. Schiff turned and saw his face. Another problem. What a hell of a time to have a migraine.

'Bright,' Bennet said.

'You want the blinds?'

Bennet nodded and Schiff leant forward, pushed a button and the blinds rolled down. Bennet groaned and leant back, holding his head.

'Turn back,' he said softly.

Schiff leant towards him, tense now, apprehensive. 'I'll book into the airport hotel,' he said, 'and we can get the next flight.'

'No.'

'John, if it's the *Register*, that's just cake icing. The *Courier* is bread and butter.'

'Turn back.'

Schiff sighed and leant forward for the intercom. More problems. He should be thriving.


A mile to the west Mike Neilson clattered his knife and fork on his plate and burped. He had put away three sausages, four rashers of bacon and two eggs, three slices of bread and a pot of tea. What he would have liked now was a few hours' kip, but the bloody reporters wouldn't let him – seemed to think they owned him, for the price of a breakfast. He got up slowly and ambled to the window.

'You met Stead a year ago?' Merton asked.

Neilson did not answer – just stood, staring through the window, then turned suddenly.

'It wasn't my fault,' he yelled.

'What wasn't?' Merton asked.

'That he was killed.'

Stone pressed the *play* button on the tape recorder as Neilson sat by the window and began to rock, like a child. 'He was all right,' he continued. 'We went together. He was all right.'

'You were lovers?' Merton asked and Neilson sneered at him, an ugly grin.

'Lovers. Shit.' Then shrugged. 'Sure. Lovers. You think he was teaching me A levels? He was all right. He was the only person who . . .' He closed his eyes for a moment, then laid the knife on the table. 'This guy,' he said, turning to look at Stone, 'in a pub. This guy. Polish. The King's Arms near the Polish Centre. Hammersmith, you know. He was a pusher. I used to get gear from him . . .'

'Heroin?' Stone asked and caught the ugly leer again.

'I'm not that stupid. Grass. He found out about Bob. One night we were drinking. He found out where Bob worked, everything. And he put the screw on me to get information from him.'

'How?' Stone asked.

'I was on a suspended for possession. All they have to do is tip the wink and you're inside.'

Merton leant forward. 'Did you get any information?' he asked.

'Sure. I got back copies of *Sanity* – you know, the CND magazine – and I pinched bits.' He stared at the ceiling and smiled. 'All GLCMs will carry a W4 counterforce warhead of two hundred and seventy pounds variable yield,' he said, then grinned at Stone. 'That sort of crap. And I made up bits and I stuck it all together and gave it to him.'

'And?' Merton asked.

The grin vanished. He hugged himself, began rocking again. 'He came back with two hundred pounds,' he said quietly. 'Cash. I knew that wasn't from the peace movement.'

'That's who he said it was for?' Merton said.

'Yes.'

'What was his name?'

'I called him "Ski". I mean, they're all bloody "skis" aren't they? He wouldn't take the money back. Well, there was no point in throwing it away, was there?' He looked from one to the other for support, pleading. Merton nodded and he continued looking hungrily at him, needing an ally. 'I didn't know what I was getting into. It was a joke. He gave me this camera. Keys that would open Bob's case. They knew he'd have papers for the Brussels meeting.'

'Who's "they"?' Merton asked.

'This Russian. Ski . . .'

'You said he was Polish.'

Neilson shook his head, a flash of irritation, flapped his hand as if brushing away a fly. 'Russian, Polish – what's the difference? He knew that Bob would have the papers for the Brussels meeting. He told me to go with him.'

'And Stead agreed?' Merton asked, trying to keep his disbelief from showing.

'You saw the ticket,' Neilson said. 'See, he wanted me out of the way and I wanted out because of Ski. So, the idea was that I would go on to a friend in Amsterdam, then, at Heathrow, it felt like a bad idea. I didn't even know if my friend would still be there. When we were through passport control, I told Bob I wanted to go with him. He told me to go back. I couldn't. I told him about Ski. Showed him the camera. And the keys. I thought he would understand, but he went mad, phoned somebody, said he had to get back, left me. I didn't know what to do, so I went to his house. When I got to

Bob's street, I saw him coming towards me. At least, I thought it was him. At first. He had the same sort of coat and trousers. He even had Bob's moustache. He was carrying the same kind of briefcase. I stopped him, then I saw it wasn't Bob. Just looked like him. He got into a car and it drove off. I went to the door and saw the keys hanging in the lock. I went in and saw him on the floor. He was staring at me. I'd never seen a dead body before. His head was cut. There was a bit of glass in it. Then I heard a noise somewhere in the house and I ran . . .'

The speech had exhausted him. He tried a smile but it was no more than a grimace.

'Why didn't you go to the police?' Merton asked.

'They would have said it was me. They couldn't bring him back. Why should I go to them? I'm so tired. I'm so bloody tired. I've been running ever since.'

'Why?' Stone asked.

'Because they're after me.'

'Who?'

'Whoever they are,' Neilson said angrily. 'Whoever wanted his papers. Because I saw the bastard who killed him.'

'Where?'

'In the bloody tube.' The words exploded out of him in a spray of spittle. 'Piccadilly. Why do you think I rang you?'

He slumped back into the seat and closed his eyes. Merton slowly got to his feet, moved towards him and gently took the knife from the table.

'I'm going to phone the office, Mike,' he said. 'I'll ask them to contact a solicitor for you.' He paused, looking down at him.

'OK, Mike?'

No response. Merton handed the knife to Stone, picked up the phone and dialled. As he reached the last digit, Neilson's eyes snapped open and he leapt from the chair. He was on to Merton in two strides, and drove a short left hook into his stomach. It was fast. Stone blinked and almost missed it. He reached out for Neilson, saw something bright flashing in front of his eyes and he stumbled back, feeling

107

blood on his cheek, then Neilson was out and there was the sound of the key turning in the lock and Stone realised what had hit him. It was the plastic tag of the room number. He'd never thought of such an innocuous thing as a weapon, but there was blood dripping on to his jacket to prove it.

For once the atmosphere of animosity between the Editor and her deputy seemed to have cleared. She paced the room, reading from a file, while he sat, papers on his lap.

' "The *Register* sets new standards in investigative reporting",' she said, and pulled a face. 'Everything sounds so corny. We need a title.' She gazed at the window, seeking inspiration. ' "Focus",' she said, and scowled. ' "Spectrum". "Behind the News".'

'Far behind the news,' Greene said. 'What about "In Depth"?'

She shook her head. 'Inside . . .'

' "Inside Story"?' Greene suggested, and she smiled and snapped her fingers. 'That's it,' she said. Greene nodded, flipped through his papers, discarded two marked 'Week in Focus' and 'Register Reports' and presented a design for 'Inside Story'. She picked it up and smiled at him. 'That's wonderful, Toby. You're a genius.'

He shrugged, attempting humility and failing. 'All we need now is a budget for it.'

'I've got the budget.'

He shook his head. 'Haven't you seen Schiff's memo?'

She frowned, turned to her desk, began sorting through an overflowing in-tray and stared at a slip of paper. ' "Freeze on editorial spending"?' she said and looked inquiringly at Greene.

'Maybe it's the strike in New York,' he suggested.

'But this is ridiculous.' She was angry again. It seemed she was forever tilting between excitement and irritation. 'Bennet passed my budget this morning.'

'Did he? What did he say?'

'He said he'd look at it, but he said it was OK. And what's Schiff doing giving the orders?'

'Par for the course,' Greene said. 'Happens so often. Someone takes over a newspaper. Grand plans – spend this, do that, until he actually has to fork out.'

'Bennet's not like that,' she said and he looked at her curiously, wondering why she was defending him. Why would she say such a thing unless the rumours had some foundation? He began packing his diagrams in a file. 'They're all like that,' he said. 'We'll be having this conversation next year and the year after . . .'

'Oh don't be so bloody defeatist, Toby,' she said, interrupting him, her anger overflowing again. 'You've got so much talent.' She pointed to the file. 'That's a lovely visual for "Inside Story". You know ten times more about design and production than I do, but you just don't believe the paper can ever get anywhere. That's why . . .' She stopped in mid-sentence.

'. . . That's why I'll never be there,' he continued for her, nodding at her chair.

'I'm sorry,' she said. 'That was clumsy of me. It's not been easy having to realise how ignorant I am.' She smiled at him, her irritation in check now, replaced by something else.

Deep down, Greene knew he would never be an editor. He knew he was no competition and briefly she felt a tremor of pity for him.

'Let's try and work together, Toby,' she said. He looked away from her, at the floor. 'I'll get the budget out of Bennet,' she said softly.

'Well,' he said, turning to go, 'you do have certain advantages over me for that.'

The same old bitchiness – she had misread his mood and her anger reared in her again and, as she snapped on the intercom, her voice was sharp: 'Angela, get me John Bennet.'

In the Grosvenor House flat, Walter Schiff was trying to make the best of things, planning what to do now that Bennet had gone sick on him. He was checking figures, working on what to say to New York, distracted by the tinkling voice of Debbie Cartwright at his side. She was apologising into the phone, then she slammed it down. Debbie never slammed the phone down. Emotion was a sign of bad breeding, but now she was petulant.

'Why can't I say he's ill?' she asked.

'And affect the share price?'

'Did he see this?' she continued, dropping a telex message on the desk. 'Forest are planning to sell the *Mercury* to Global. There won't be a print contract for us.' He ignored it, but she would not keep quiet. Something was bothering her. 'Aren't you going to tell him?' she asked.

'I'm behind on my insurance payments,' he quipped. But she did not laugh.

'The telex was here when you came up to see if the contract had arrived.'

'Was it?'

'Look at the time slug.' She pushed it in front of him again.

'We had a plane to catch,' he said. 'I didn't check this.' He looked at her. She gazed back at him, and shook her head. 'Don't you believe me?' he asked.

'You don't always act in his best interests,' she said, and as the words came out she knew it was a mistake. He pounced on her, finger stabbing at her face, making her back away.

'He sometimes doesn't know what his best interests are,' he said. 'Where do you think he gets his money from? The *Register*?' Then he moved to the window, shaking his head. 'I don't know why he's so hot on the paper. I thought it would be a flash in the pan but he's spending money on it. My money included.' He turned. 'Ever read Drucker?' She shook her head, scared of him. She'd never seen the little man show emotion. He was the dry one, the figures man, the little guy with a calculator for a brain.

'Some properties generate income,' he continued. 'Most generate costs. You not only have to make money. You have to

110

keep it. By throwing away. I'm the trash man around here.' He pointed to his chest, then to the bedroom. 'I think of nothing else but his best interests.'

There was a knock at the door. Schiff opened it.

A waiter came in with coffee and a sandwich. Schiff nodded to the bedroom. The waiter went to the door, knocked gently and went inside. A moment later there was a yell, Bennet's voice roaring: 'Get out,' and the waiter was back in the room, red-faced, embarrassed. In the darkness he had tripped over something. Spilt coffee dripped from the tray. Schiff pulled his money clip from his back pocket and laid a five-pound note on the tray. 'Sorry,' he said. 'Nothing personal. He has a migraine.' He winked at the man. 'No chatter, OK?'

The waiter nodded and Schiff neatly picked up the sandwich, took a bite and closed the door behind the man.

'What is it?' Debbie asked, eyes bright, looking at the bedroom door.

'Maybe he wanted brown bread,' Schiff said and chuckled to himself, then pointed to the film poster. 'His wife's been dead nearly five years and still she's trouble.'

'What happened?' Debbie asked. 'When she killed herself?'

'She didn't. Accidental overdose.'

Then Bennet called his name and asked him to close the bedroom door. He did so, gently, and looked up at the poster again. 'It happened on his son's birthday,' he said. 'Coming up. In two days' time.'

In Paula's office, David Stone tenderly touched the band-aid on his face and winced. He was uncomfortable and sore, his News Editor on his left and his Editor standing over him. He was glad at least that Merton had been with him. He would have felt even more foolish if he'd got himself locked in a hotel room on his own and lost his contact. At least there was Merton to share the embarrassment.

'The police slapped my wrist,' he said to Paula. 'This

111

Superintendant Hammerton. Hard bastard. He reckons Neilson's dangerous. He's got previous. GBH. Hammerton reckons I'm lucky to get away with this.' He touched the plaster on his cheek again. 'He told me to stick to writing stories in future.'

Paula looked at him and began pacing the room. 'Hammerton thinks Neilson's the killer,' Stone continued. 'I asked him about Stead's briefcase but he said it was in the house.'

'How much of the story did you believe?' Merton asked.

'About half.'

'Which half?'

'The half that says he was out for what he could get. I don't think he was an unwilling spy. Maybe he even set it up. There have been rumours of leaks for a year. That's when Neilson first met Stead. That night, when he confessed to Stead . . .'

'Or was found out,' Merton suggested.

'Right. If Ski is the one running Neilson, he's not going to leave it to him, is he? When Stead goes home, he's followed. Struggle. Heart attack. They arrange it to look like an accident, but Neilson appears, sees someone . . .'

'If he's speaking the truth,' Paula said. 'He said the briefcase was missing. We can check that.'

'With the police?' Stone said, grinning, shaking his head. 'I don't think . . .'

'With Mrs Stead,' Paula said.

'She's gone to ground,' Merton said.

'She's back,' Paula said. 'She's selling the house. Bright boy on the local paper just phoned.'

Stone got to his feet, excited again, reaching for his notebook. 'I'll go,' he said, but Paula stopped him, a hand on his chest.

'In the morning. Go home. Cool off.' He shrugged, deflated. 'And David,' she continued. 'I don't want any more trouble from the police. I came close to withholding information this morning and I'm not carrying another can. Don't do anything stupid.'

The phone rang. Merton picked it up, grunted into it and handed it to Paula. She grabbed it and frowned. 'Well, can I speak to Schiff, Debbie . . .? There's writers I've contacted . . . I'll lose them as well as looking like an idiot. What the hell is going on . . .?'

The answer did not satisfy her. She slammed the phone down, reached for her jacket and went out, muttering dark curses.

Fifteen minutes later she knocked on the door of Bennet's flat, expecting to see Debbie. The young woman always seemed to be around, either at the office or the flat. Maybe she was more than a PA to him, Paula wondered, then dismissed the idea. She was becoming as bad as the gossips in the Feathers, adding two and two and making eight, and it was Schiff who answered.

'I want to see him,' she said, striding in without waiting to be invited.

'You can't,' he said. 'Migraine. Like everything else, he goes in for it in a big way.'

'And you're in charge?'

'Who else?'

She stared at him for a moment. 'You can't cancel my budget, Walter,' she said quietly.

'Suspend it,' he said.

'Why?'

'The paper's on the critical list.'

'Rubbish,' she snapped. 'We've met every target. Circulation, advertising. Production.'

'I know,' he conceded. 'You're going like a bomb. But we've lost the *Mercury* print contract.' She sat heavily against the desk, mouth open, blinking at him. 'They're selling the paper to Global,' he continued. 'And the strike in New York doesn't help. Sorry, Paula.'

She looked up at him, suddenly vulnerable, like a kid who's just been told there's no Santa Claus.

'What's going to happen?' she asked.

'At worst, no expansion. At best, trim . . .'

113

He stopped as a groan seeped through the bedroom door, then a yell: 'Debbie! Someone! Jesus!'

He was through the door fast. Paula followed him and stood in the doorway peering in through the gloom. Bennet had knocked over a glass of water. He was stumbling around the room as if he were blind, mumbling questions. 'Debbie gone? Yes. Time? Half-six. Might make the ten o'clock . . .' Then he looked up, peered at the door. 'Who's that?'

'Paula,' said Schiff.

'Paula. What the hell . . .' He reached for a bottle of pills and bumped the water jug again with his elbow. She marched in and picked it up.

'I can manage,' he said.

'You can't,' she said, poured a glass of water and guided it to his mouth. He took a pill and lay back on the bed. 'My mother had bad attacks,' she said and stepped back. He was lying on the bed now, fully clad, his shoes on, the laces tied.

'Why don't you just rest?' she said. 'If you're determined to catch the ten o'clock, the attack will just get worse.'

'He has to,' Schiff said. 'There's a bloody strike on.'

She looked from one to the other – Schiff anxious, Bennet in agony.

'Can you sit up?' she asked.

He struggled into a sitting position and she arranged the pillows for him.

'I can't stand people seeing me like this,' he said.

'Why?' Paula asked – but she knew the answer.

# Twelve

As he paid off the taxi, David Stone wondered if he was doing the right thing. Paula would be angry, but if he got what he wanted, she would forgive him – he hoped. Anyway, it was worth a try. No one got anywhere in this game without taking risks. She knew that, more than most. She would forgive him.

There was a light on in Number Eight. He took a deep breath and rang the bell. A moment later a woman opened it. This would be her, he thought. Mid-thirties, maybe; attractive. Even as she spoke, his mind was asking him questions. Why in God's name would a man like Stead prefer a little bender like Neilson to a woman like this?

'Mrs Stead. David Stone, *Sunday Register*.'

'Oh God.' Her hand fluttered to her mouth.

'I've just talked to . . .'

'Go away!'

'. . . Mike Neilson.'

She shook her head, hand on the door ready to close it. 'I can't help you,' she said.

'I'd like to check what Neilson told me about your husband.'

The door was almost closed on him. An inch of light in his eyes. Then it opened again. 'Mind the carpet there,' she said. 'It's loose.'

The living-room reminded Stone of his old aunt's in the country. Flowered chair covers, copies of *Country Life* on the coffee table, photographs of children on the mantlepiece. An old-fashioned walnut bureau stood in the corner. It was open. Papers were scattered on the counter. A briefcase lay in one corner.

'They found him there,' she said, pointing at the coffee table. She seemed perfectly composed, as if pointing to some favourite piece of furniture. It was a brave attempt and Stone was not fooled, but he had to take his chance and get in his questions while he had it.

'Was his briefcase missing?'

'What?' She looked at him, confused, then followed his gaze to the corner.

'Is that his?' he asked.

'Yes.' She stared hard at him for a moment as if trying to guess what he was thinking. 'Mr Stone,' she said. 'Get one thing into your head. My husband was not a spy. Nor was he careless with his papers. That briefcase is old. It wasn't the one he was using.'

'Where is it?'

'The police have it.'

'Have you seen it?'

'No.'

'Did they give you a receipt for it?'

'I can't remember.' She turned away from him, bored with his questions. There was only one thing that interested her. 'What did Neilson say about my husband?'

'That he had an affair with him.' Even as he said it, the word sounded odd. Affair. It was a cobwebbed word, ancient, nothing to do with the Eighties.

'Sexual?' she said and for a moment he thought she was going to laugh. 'What rubbish. What fantastic rubbish! My husband took pity on people. It wasn't so much generosity, as guilt about his own good fortune. That was his problem, Mr Stone. Lame ducks. He got involved with Neilson because he was trying to get him out of his miserable squat into a room somewhere.'

'Where was that? The squat?'

'How should I know?' She turned and moved to the

116

bureau. 'I suppose until he's found, you'll go on inventing lurid stories?' She picked up a piece of paper. It was lined, and torn from a notebook. From his position by the door he could see scrawls – possibly a list of addresses. 'I've been clearing out,' she said.

He crossed the room and looked at the piece of paper over her shoulder. She was trembling, as if she was about to cry.

'Have you shown this to the police?' he asked.

She shook her head. The tears were not far away and she was fighting for self-control. She handed him the piece of paper. 'I've only just found out,' she said quietly. As he took a note of the addresses, she said in a small voice, 'Will you do your best for me?'

'I'll report what you say,' he said, then pointed to a photograph on the mantelpiece, a family snap in a park – the Steads and their children. 'Could I borrow this?'

'Yes, I suppose so.' Then she stiffened and shook her head. 'No. I don't want that. No photographs. I'm sorry. We were married for fifteen years. We were happy. I don't suppose that's news, is it?' She turned and looked up at him, pleading. 'Do believe me, Mr Stone, or you'll get it all terribly, terribly wrong. He was not a spy, nor was he –' she paused, 'awful word – gay.'


She had been with him for an hour, watching him, thinking of the days not long ago when she had sat with her mother. It was awful. Migraine was debilitating. It could turn strong people into weeping babies. Then he grunted and came slowly awake.

'Have I been asleep?'

She nodded.

He looked over her shoulder at Schiff in the doorway. 'He's afraid you're another Anna. My wife. Aren't you, Walter?'

Paula turned, and saw Schiff looking at her. 'To this company, he's blood,' he said, nodding at Bennet. 'She was a

117

haemorrhage.' He looked at his watch. 'We've still time to get the ten o'clock.'

'Get the lady a drink,' Bennet said.

'I don't want one,' Paula replied.

'Give her a bourbon, my way,' he insisted. She smiled. He was improving. The pills were beginning to work. She knew the signs. He was becoming his old, dominant, obnoxious self. 'With fresh lemon and ice,' he said to Schiff, then turned to her. 'Anna was an actress, a bit-part hooker. I made her a great actress – nearly.'

'I came about the budget,' Paula said, but he continued as if she hadn't spoken. 'She treated me like dirt. She had a skin so pale you could see through it. She enjoyed life like a child. I've never been so happy as when the sun suddenly shone after bad weather and she said, "Let's take off." Once we bought an oil-well because she wanted to see it gush.'

Christ, she thought, what *is* this? Then he opened his eyes and smiled that godammed infectious smile of his. 'I bought her a movie,' he said. ' "Summer." She really hit it in that. Did you see it?'

'She was lovely,' Paula said. It was what he wanted to hear and, besides, it was no lie.

'She was,' he said, 'but she couldn't repeat it. She tried to kill herself. I watched her, but you can't watch all the time. The next time she tried to kill our son, then herself. So, when the next time came, I let her do it. I made sure she had the right dose and wasn't interrupted.'

He had turned away from her and suddenly she wanted to comfort him. It was cliché time again and she knew it, but he had opened up to her and something in her wanted to respond. Then there was a clink of ice behind her and she turned to see Schiff with her drink, and she was glad of the interruption.

'Your budget,' Bennet said. 'What about your budget?'

Schiff told him about the contract.

'Why the hell didn't you tell me before?' Bennet asked. He

was improving. The anger was back which meant that the migraine was on the retreat.

'How could I?' Schiff said. 'You were in no state.'

'Christ,' Bennet roared. 'What were you going to do? Tell me on the plane?'

Schiff shrugged, handed Paula her drink and went back to the office. Bennet slowly got to his feet and followed him, with Paula a pace behind.

Schiff turned. 'You OK?'

'I can see you all right, yes.'

'The car's waiting.'

'You go,' Bennet said. 'You've always reckoned you could run this business better than me. You settle the strike. And you'd better do it.'

Schiff looked at him suspiciously. 'What are you going to do?'

'Rest. Like the lady says.'

'The *Register*'s not viable without that print contract,' Schiff insisted.

'I'm not going to throw away a great paper.'

'Great paper!'

For a moment Paula thought he was going to spit on the carpet in contempt. She picked up her coat. She didn't need this.

'You stay,' Bennet said. 'Learn something about the business.'

'John,' Schiff said, anger mingled now with a pleading tone. 'The stockholders aren't going to stand much more.'

'Sod the stockholders. I still have control.'

'If you keep throwing money away here . . .'

'Stop worrying,' Bennet said, closing on Schiff. Paula could almost smell the anger in him. 'I'll fix the *Mercury* contract.'

'How?' Schiff spread his arms, exasperated. 'We can't afford a strike over there and losses over here. Look, John, we can handle it, but it has to be together.' The two men were

119

head to head now and Paula felt excluded. She wanted to go but they were at the door, blocking her exit. 'You with the people,' Schiff was saying, 'me with the small print.' Then he leant closer and whispered, and she could hardly hear what he was saying, 'Why do you have to buy them a movie? A newspaper? Why don't you just . . .?'

Then Bennet grabbed him by the lapels, suddenly and brutally pulling him upright, stretching him, the little man's feet almost off the floor. Bennet held him for a moment, then pushed him away.

'You'll just about make it, Walter,' he said.

Schiff smoothed down his jacket, picked up his briefcase, opened the door and looked at Paula for a moment, and she felt like Anna Bennet must have felt, like an outsider, like – what had Schiff called her? – a haemorrhage.

Now he could see perfectly and the pain was not so intense. She handed him a copy of the *Standard*. Neilson's photograph was on the front under the headline: *Stead – Man Wanted*.

Bennet was impressed. 'You've got an interview with him, on ice? Christ!'

'But we can't follow this unless . . .'

'I know, I know.'

'Solicitors cost a fortune, but the money's only a drop in the ocean compared with . . .'

'I can't ignore Walter,' he said. 'We're not inseparable, but our money is. He's written a minimum-loss clause into the UK business and, if that operates, there's nothing I can do, unless . . .'

'What?'

He smiled at her. 'I'll find a way. For you.'

'I'd rather you did it for the paper.'

He picked up the cocktail shaker and rattled the ice. She shook her head, but he poured two glasses nonetheless.

'Are you happy?' he asked.

'*Happy?*'

120

'There's something wrong with the word?'

No response.

'Oh come on, Paula,' he said. 'Don't be so stiff, English, buttoned up. Just look at yourself.' He took her by the arm and guided her to the bedroom, positioned her in front of the mirror. 'Look. Six months ago you gawked across the Dorchester to get your award in some hand-me-down dress that had split across here . . .' He drew his hand across her stomach and she laughed ' . . . like a girl fresh out of school,' he continued. 'And now look at you. You've found yourself.'

He was gazing at her in the mirror and she let herself be drawn round towards him and permitted herself to be kissed. It wasn't unpleasant. It wasn't a problem. Then she broke from him, went back to the office and looked at the film poster.

'I suppose you've been setting me up in the same sort of way?' she said.

'Too neat.'

'Something of that?'

He shook his head. 'You were business. A chance I took. That's all. You came in against the odds.' Again he turned her towards him. 'Everyone thinks we're sleeping together.'

'Except me.'

She moved away, slugged back the remains of her drink and moved to the door.

'Stay,' he said.

'Is that an order?'

'A request.'

She turned. 'To answer your question, no, I'm not happy. Half the time I'm so exhilarated, half the time so tired, yet I wake up in the middle of the night and all I can think about is the baby.'

'I'd forgotten about that,' he said.

'Well *I* haven't.' And she went out fast, half running along the corridor, cursing herself, her stupid Florence Nightingale instinct which had almost caught her off guard.

121

By the time she had got to the car, she had composed herself. She had decided to go straight home. There was a pile of reading to be done, but the car-phone was bleeping yellow light at her. She picked it up. It was Alan Merton.

'It's David,' he said. 'Silly young bastard. He's found Neilson again, dead this time, a needle sticking out of his arm . . .'

She battered him with questions, and all the answers were the wrong ones. Then she slammed down the phone, checked her A-Z, bucketed the car away from the kerb and drove north along Park Lane towards Notting Hill. At first her reaction was anger. Why hadn't the young fool done what she'd told him? What was he doing scuffling around the slums at this time of night, keeping everyone out of their beds? A corpse! A seedy squat in Notting Hill! She shuddered. Merton had tried for levity. At least, he'd said, when Stone found the body, he'd had the gumption to phone him first. Merton had done the right thing, told Stone to go back to the body and wait, then he had called the police.

It took her ten minutes along the Bayswater Road and right into Ladbroke Grove, up the hill past the expensive houses and down into the badlands. Checking left and right, she was reminded again of London as a Jekyll and Hyde city, one street all prettified, the next a tinned-up slum of derelict houses and derelict people. A right and two lefts and she was suddenly in the right place. She drew up behind a police car and an ambulance; blue lights revolved, illuminating a crowd of rubberneckers. As she got out, she spotted Merton strolling towards her.

'He's still up there,' he said.

'Silly sod,' she said.

'Quite.'

They reached the house just as the front door opened and Stone was led out between two policemen, tall, heavy men, scowling.

'The one on the left is Hammerton,' Merton said. Paula nodded and pushed through the crowd towards them. Stone smiled, a crooked grin in a white face.

'I'm Paula Croxley,' she said to Hammerton. 'Editor of the paper. Can I talk to him?'

'No,' said Hammerton.

'Where are you taking him?'

'Notting Hill.'

They pushed Stone into the car and she leant in, told him she would get a lawyer, then turned to Hammerton. 'He just found the body. You can't think he's involved. Why don't you . . .'

'You're both involved,' Hammerton said, slamming the door and looking up at her through the open window. 'Withholding that sort of information.'

'What information?'

'He knew where to find Neilson.'

'He's just a good reporter,' she said, running as the car eased away from the kerb.

'If you'd told us what you knew,' Hammerton said over his shoulder, 'that poor sod would be alive today.'

The car drove off and Paula watched it go, then wandered across to her car, Merton behind her.

'There's nothing we could have done,' he said.

She glared at him. 'He should have phoned Hammerton.'

'Would you?' he asked softly.

'He might have been killed,' she shouted. 'I never took stupid risks like that.'

'And you always used to phone in.'

She opened her door and climbed in.

'At least he's given us a good start for "Inside Story",' Merton said.

'And a good finish. I haven't got the budget, Alan.'

She explained, then added, 'And I won't play his game.'

'What game?'

She merely shrugged. 'Will you phone the lawyer, Alan, and get that fool out of the nick?'

And she drove off fast, leaving Merton standing in the gutter with more questions than answers.

123

# Thirteen

Alan Merton got into the office early, looking forward to the day's work. Maybe there would be trouble – perhaps the paper might find itself in bother with the law but this was better than the old days of going through the motions. There was a story here, maybe not as strong a story as Stone suspected, but there was a story nonetheless. He smiled to himself as he climbed the stairs. Young Stone would have had a bad night. He'd been silly and impetuous and he needed cooling off, but he would rather have one silly, impetuous, enthusiastic young reporter than ten cynics who thought only about the train home to Orpington.

Fowler was already at his desk and Merton smiled again. Orpington. Fowler was from Orpington. Jim Fowler would never spend a night in jail in pursuit of a story. They had hardly had time to exchange good mornings when Bennet breezed into the room, smiling at them, snapping his fingers.

'Remember what I said, Alan,' Bennet said. 'Quote: "If a dead body were found on these steps some other paper would carry the story first." Unquote. Remember? Check it and use it in the story, why don't you? Now at least we're finding the bodies.' He looked around the empty room. 'Where's Stone?'

'With Paula,' Merton said.

'They let him go?' Merton thought he caught a trace of disappointment in the man's voice.

'Eventually,' he said.

'Pity.' He grinned. 'That could have been a runner.' He

turned to go and shouted over his shoulder, 'Tell Stone to keep finding them.'

Merton watched him go and shook his head. 'He's cheerful.'

'Obvious,' Fowler said. 'He's selling out. I knew he wouldn't get the *Mercury* contract. Soon there will be another egomaniac charging through here, spilling blood.'

Merton looked up, saw Paula waving at him, and he got to his feet. The Editor wanted him. Right, he thought, let's go. Let's get this tale sorted out.

Stone was leaning against the wall in Paula's office, hands wrapped around a mug of coffee. He looked bad – like a guy who had seen a corpse, then spent a night in the nick. Paula sat at her desk, listening intently as Stone went over his story.

'Neilson must have been dead by the time Mrs Stead gave me those addresses. Hammerton's going insane because they're covering up and I got there first.'

'It can't have been a coincidence she just found those addresses,' Merton said.

'No. She was keeping them from the police in the hope that that side of her husband's life would go away.'

'Then why give them to you?' Paula asked.

'I don't know. Maybe because Neilson was in the *Standard*. She could see it was all going to come out. Maybe in a funny way she wanted it to come out. There's something she's keeping back, or frightened of. Yes, that's right. She was very controlled, but underneath, frightened.'

There was a knock on the door and Greene came in with a piece of agency copy. He handed it to Paula. 'I thought you should see this,' he said. 'Please don't shoot the messenger if it spoils the story.'

Paula read it and looked up. 'It's the police statement on Neilson,' she said, then read aloud: ' "Preliminary medical evidence . . . no sign of force on the body . . . injection consistent with being self-administrated . . . over-dosage not massive and could have been accidental." ' She looked at

Stone. 'They're not ruling out murder.'

Stone snatched it from her, spilling coffee. 'Not ruling it out!' he yelled. 'Hammerton knows he was murdered.'

'Does he now?' said Greene.

Stone turned on him and waved the copy in his face. 'The whole place was in a panic last night. Hammerton was going mad. Why? Because Neilson overdosed?' He shook his head at the absurdity of it. 'There'll be another adjourned inquest. This is another Stead.'

'On the other hand,' said Greene slowly and precisely, deliberately calm, 'it could just possibly be an accidental overdose.'

'Bollocks,' said Stone.

'You *want* Neilson to be murdered, that's all,' said Greene.

'And you want the story to be a dud,' Stone replied. 'You want the paper to be a dud.'

A stand-off. Paula stepped between them, telling Stone to shut up and apologising to Greene. 'He's tired,' she said.

Greene wouldn't be pacified. He turned to go. 'I think we're tired. It may be clouding our judgment.'

He went out and Stone stared angrily at the door. 'Clouding our judgment,' he repeated. 'It couldn't be any clearer. Neilson didn't use heroin.'

'He said,' said Merton.

'Did you see any needle-marks?' Paula asked.

'You mean, when I did the autopsy?' he said, sarcastically.

'Did you see any needle-marks?' Paula repeated.

He shook his head and crumpled on to a chair. 'I'm stupid,' he said. 'I just saw him and I gagged and ran.'

Paula looked at Merton. 'Can you remember? In the hotel? The backs of his hands?'

'I'm not sure,' he said. 'Anyway, it cuts both ways. If he didn't use, then it's murder. If he did, he knew enough not to overdose.'

'Unless he meant to,' she said. 'And there's always a risk.'

'Oh, Paula,' Stone said in desperation. 'It's all too much of a coincidence. Neilson found dead now. The police won't produce Stead's document case. Neilson's Polish contact.'

'At least we can check that,' Paula said. 'Maybe the bar staff in the pub saw Neilson with the Pole.'

Stone got to his feet. 'Right I'll . . .'

'. . . get some sleep,' Paula said.

He nodded and went to the door, then turned, bright-eyed again. He'd just thought of something. 'We haven't a picture of Mrs Stead,' he said, then he was out and running again.

Paula briefly made a move to stop him, then changed her mind. Maybe David Stone needed some sleep, but there were times when she had needed sleep. Many a story would have gone to the opposition because a reporter slept on the job . . . Then the phone rang and she put David Stone out of her mind. Bennet wanted to see her. She grinned at Merton, gave a little mock salute and led him out of the room.

Bennet wanted to know what they were doing with the story and he wasn't impressed by her caution.

'Not clear?' he said. 'What do you mean, "Not clear"?'

'It's not even clear if anyone was murdered.' Now it was she who was calm in the face of his wild enthusiasm.

'Of course they were murdered,' he said. 'By the Russians.'

'How do you know?'

'It's going to be in my American papers this morning, that's how I know. The CIA knew all about Stead and Neilson.'

The CIA? She didn't believe him. The trouble was, half the time she didn't believe a word he said. 'Then why didn't they tell us?' she asked.

'Maybe they did. Maybe someone over here ballsed it up. Maybe the CIA wanted it to happen.'

Curiouser and curiouser. Now she was baffled.

'Look,' he said. 'Stead had access to information on US bases. There's a group in Washington that would like everything in every US base in this country stamped *For American eyes only*. Something like this gives them their golden opportunity . . .'

'All right,' she said. 'If they've both been murdered, we're saying there's been a gigantic cover-up.'

127

'Of course there's been a cover-up.' He sounded exasperated now at her inability to comprehend. 'It stinks. Don't you think it stinks?'

'Yes, but if the Russians murdered them, why are the police protecting them?'

He lost patience. 'Don't be so naive,' he snapped. 'The police aren't protecting them. All they care about is saying Stead wasn't a spy, that there were no leaks and there's nothing to worry Anglo-US relations.' He scribbled on a pad and tore off a piece of paper. 'Here's a number in Washington. There are one or two loose ends. Tie them up. Put everyone you can on it.'

'That won't be many,' she said, taking it and glancing at the name. It meant nothing to her.

'Christ,' he said. 'When I went into newspapers, we dug out major scandals with one man and a boy. Now it takes a whole army.' He looked at her. She was dubious. 'Come on,' he said. 'What are you worried about? It's a great story.'

'But is it *true*?'

'Who cares? It's all in quotes. I'm bumping up the print-run by twenty per cent. I've booked television ads. The story exposes the evils of Communism. These bastards think they can murder people and get away with it, and this Government is in collusion.' He held up a copy of the paper and gazed at imaginary headlines. 'Once again democracy depends on the free press.' Then he began scrabbling among the chaos on his desk. 'What the hell am I looking for?' For a moment he was distracted. 'Last night . . .' he said.

'Yes?'

'I was ill. Not myself. Nothing happened.' He wasn't looking at her.

'Nothing happened so far as I was concerned.'

'Good. Right.' Then he found what he was looking for and handed over a sheaf of papers. 'Your budget.'

She looked at it and frowned.

'What's wrong?' he asked. 'It's not enough?'

'It's enough.'

'I should bloody well hope so. I'm spending five million on you, two million on bigger issues and editorial expansion, and three million on promotion.'

She turned to go and he called out to her, 'When I was a child, I was taught to say thank you.'

'Thank you,' she said and turned to look at him. She was baffled. None of this squared with Schiff's pessimism of last night. Unless . . . 'Have you got the print contract?' she asked.

'No.' He smiled and pointed to a copy of the *Mercury* on his desk. 'So I'm buying the paper.'

# Fourteen

They had stood the story up a little. Archie had confirmed the fact that Neilson regularly met a Pole in the Hammersmith pub; and Morris had taken shots of Mrs Stead coming out of her house with a man Stone later identified as Andrew Osbourne, Under Secretary at the Ministry of Defence and Stead's boss; and so, by rights, Paula should have been exhilarated. By most of the rules of journalism, she had a great story. The television advert had been a success. It was a montage of Neilson's face with a voice-over asking the question, 'Spy or dupe?' and the taster for the readers that he had talked to *Register* reporters on his last day alive.

There were eight extra pages, including two full-page ads sold on the back of the story – thirty thousand pounds' worth of space and a hundred thousand extra copies, and the old Goss had managed to crank them all out.

She should have been exhilarated, but she was worried. She knew, deep down, that they didn't have enough. Her instincts were at war with each other. Part of her, the new responsible Editor part, wanted to be cautious, to agree with Toby Greene. The other part said the hell with it, publish and be damned, and that Tuesday morning, as she drove to work with the paper on the passenger seat, the responsible part of her had gained ground and she wondered maybe if she was cut out for the job. She thought back to the good old days when she was on the road and it was someone else's responsibility to make decisions on her copy.

Merton, dear dependable Merton, was, as usual, the

friendly ear. They were alone in the newsroom – the early birds – and he was listening to her grumbling.

'I'm still not an editor.'

'Why?' he asked. 'Because Bennet put his oar in?'

'Partly. Partly because I'm still a reporter. In my bones. I saw David's face and I thought, what the hell, I've had enough stories killed by cautious editors.'

'So what are you worried about?'

She shrugged, then looked up as Fowler came shambling towards them, smiling, throwing his jacket at his chair. 'Another Tuesday,' he said. 'I hate Tuesdays.' Then grinned. 'Morning folks. Terrific issue.'

'Don't you think it was all conjecture?' Paula asked.

'No. In the pub on Sunday I really felt someone you know. With my friends. Civilians. I felt terrific.'

'We're on question time in the House,' Merton said.

'Right. You got to hand it to Bennet. He really makes things happen. Even on a Tuesday, taking over the *Mercury* . . .'

'I don't know where he's getting the money from,' Paula said. 'Last week we were broke.'

'He'll get it,' Fowler said.

'You have one of your feelings?' Merton asked.

Fowler nodded. 'You know, for the first time since Wapping, do you know what I feel?'

'What?'

'Secure.'


Walter Schiff came out of Terminal Three at a run, clutching a briefcase in one hand and his overnight bag in the other. He ignored the queue for cabs and went straight to the front. His luck was in. The driver was Jewish and the woman about to get in was old.

'Would you mind,' he said, gently easing his way in front of her. 'My father's dying.' The old woman offered condolences. Schiff thanked her and climbed in. '*Sunday Register*,' he said.

'The *Register*'s a hospital now?' said the driver.

'For sick newspapers, yeah. Ten on top if you move it.'

The M4 was clear. There was a slight build-up at Chiswick and the Hammersmith flyover, and Schiff silently cursed, kept checking his watch, feeding his ulcer with anxiety. At a set of lights he noticed the *Daily Mercury* lying crushed beside the handbrake.

'That your regular paper?' he asked.

The driver shook his head. 'I pick that up from the bins. It's the old lady's bingo sheet. Wouldn't buy it.'

Schiff nodded. A fair appraisal, he reckoned. He was silent for the rest of the trip, and when they reached the office he was fast out of the cab, into the lift, and quickly through the door into Debbie's office. She looked up and automatically reached for the intercom.

'Don't announce me,' he said. 'I want to be a nice surprise.' And he went into Bennet's office without knocking.

Bennet was on the phone, his back turned, and at first he did not notice the little man. 'OK,' he was saying, 'thirty million. I was bidding high. And you reckon you can underwrite that . . .? Sure, subject to the usual . . . thanks.' He put the phone down and turned. 'Walter,' he said, getting to his feet. 'I thought you were in New York. The strike . . .'

'The agreement's signed,' Schiff said.

'Good. You shouldn't have rushed back.'

'I thought you might need me.'

Bennet grinned, shook Schiff's hand. 'As a matter of fact I do. While you were away, I had an inspiration . . .'

Schiff pulled the *Mercury* from his coat pocket. 'If you can't print it, buy it,' he said.

'You had the same thought.' Bennet's smile broadened. He was happy, exultant, doing what he was best at, but Schiff wasn't sharing in the euphoria.

'A readership of geriatrics?' Schiff said.

'So it's cheap.'

'Bingo?'

'On the way out. It's in profit, even with that.'

'A thirty million stock issue, and how much from the bank?'

132

'Twenty.'

'Fifty million,' said Schiff mournfully.

'It's the answer.' Bennet picked up a thick sheaf of papers bound in red from his desk and waved it at him. 'Read the analysis. I have another call to make.'

Schiff took it and spun it back onto the desk. It skidded on the mahogany and sprayed papers onto the carpet. 'You must be nuts,' he said. 'You must be crazy about her. Remember, I've seen it all before.'

Bennet's smile vanished. 'Watch your mouth, Walter,' he said softly, but Schiff wouldn't shut up.

'Why don't you buy her a paper in the mid-West, or a yacht, or a palace or something? She comes round to your flat, opens her legs and you . . .'

He'd gone over the top. Bennet sprang at him and he ducked away behind a chair. Bennet came after him, throwing the chair out of the way, both fists clenched. He had Schiff in a corner now but the little man wasn't about to fall. 'You better let me finish,' he said. Bennet stood motionless. 'In New York I saw our biggest stockholder.' He made a mock bow. 'After you, of course. They're worried about the effect the UK is having on profits.'

'I'll fix Ed,' Bennet said dismissively.

'Not any more.' He reached into his briefcase, produced an envelope and handed it over.

'Why doesn't he call me if he's that worried?' Bennet said.

'Because you never tell him what's going on.'

Bennet threw the letter on to the desk and picked up the phone.

'I wouldn't,' said Schiff. Bennet turned, the phone held by his side, quietly purring. 'There's been a change in the rules, John,' Schiff said quietly. 'You run this outfit because Ed's fifteen per cent plus your thirty give you effective control. He's with you, but he's no longer a dumb block of votes.'

Bennet replaced the receiver. 'And with your two-point-one per cent,' he said slowly, 'you're the power broker, are you?'

133

'He trusts me.'

'He trusts *you*?' Bennet's voice was curdled with sarcasm. He walked to the window. Behind him, Schiff lit a cigarette. The very sound of it made Bennet turn in a rage; the fact that Schiff was so much in control made him want to punch the little man's lights out. Instead he went back to the desk and picked up the analysis. Figures were figures. Figures were what Schiff was all about.

'Will you read this, Walter?' he asked quietly.

'What's the point?'

'We're committed.'

'Committed?' Schiff's eyes widened. 'How can you be? We haven't made the bid yet.'

'I've authorised five million dollars of expenditure on the *Register*,' he explained. 'And that makes no sense unless we take over the *Mercury*.'

'Five million!' Schiff was no longer in control.

'That's the spend.'

'You can't do that.'

'I've done it,' Bennet said calmly. 'Space has been booked.'

'Cancel it.'

'Staff are being hired.'

'Fire them.'

Bennet shook his head. 'I can't.'

'You've got to.'

*You've got to.* The phrase shattered Bennet's composure. No one said *you've got to* do anything to John Bennet. No one ever had. Not for years. No one told him what to do. Never. He spoke softly. 'Don't you tell me what I can and can't do with my own business, you lousy, corrupt, two-timing bastard. Get out.'

Schiff made for the door and opened it. 'I'll fix Ed,' Bennet said to his back, 'then I'll fix you. I'll break you in this business . . .' Schiff passed by Debbie's desk, then heard his name called. He turned. He knew what Bennet was thinking. The man couldn't let his anger get the better of his mathematics. Fifteen per cent. Thirty per cent. Two-and-a-half per cent. Those were the numbers that counted. He turned. Bennet was at the door, looking at Debbie.

'Put the *Mercury* on the back burner,' he said. 'And no calls.' The door was opened again to Schiff. It had to be. Bennet had no choice. Schiff walked back in, took a seat and waited for the apology.

'Walter,' said Bennet at last. 'I'm grateful to you.'

Another pause. Schiff waited.

'Clearly,' Bennet said, 'if one of our major stockholders is unhappy, we have to take that on board.' He offered a drink. 'Bourbon, my way?'

'Scotch.'

'Scotch?' Bennet said, surprised.

'I always hated bourbon, your way.' Now that he was a power broker, Walter Schiff would drink what he liked. No more bourbon with crunched bloody ice and bloody lemon. Plus, Bennet could get it for him. He was sick of being a gofer. Bennet poured, threw in a handful of cubes and looked down at him.

'What do we do if we don't expand?' he asked.

'Sell out.' The answer to Schiff was obvious.

'Have you worked out what the loss would be?'

'A damn sight less than continuing.'

'As we are, yes. We've just had a damaging strike. We pull out here, our stock price on Wall Street goes down. Boy, that's the loss, Walter.'

'Paper,' said Schiff.'

Bennet shook his head. 'No. We've just pulled up our seed-corn. What do we recover on? My plan could work. The unions are on the run. We can really get on the new technology gravy-train, just as I predicted when we first came here. With our American experience. God, I did all this when I first went to the States. We'll soon pull ahead of the others. Fast press, running seven days a week. Colour. Print in Birmingham for centralised distribution. Sell this place.' He picked up the analysis. 'Read it. There are big profits.'

'And big risks.'

'But not for you, Walter. You say to Ed: "I've gone into it further. Going back is as risky as going on. I think we should give Bennet one more chance." ' He paused. Schiff was thinking. Bennet could tell. The little man's fingers were moving, like he was working an imaginary calculus. 'Think, Walter. We make it, we make it. We don't, I lose. He'll switch his votes. You'll have what you've always wanted.' He pointed to the leather armchair behind the desk. 'What do you have to lose?'

Schiff reached for the analysis, then his fingers twitched and he pulled his hand back. 'The Monopolies Commission,' he said. 'The other bidder doesn't have to worry about it. If we're referred, it's curtains.'

Bennet shrugged. 'We buy a few MPs. No problem.'

Schiff looked at him for a moment, then leant forward, picked up the analysis and opened it. 'What's the catch?' he asked.

'You tell me, Walter. You're the lawyer.'

By late afternoon, Paula's apprehensions had been confirmed. The Home Secretary had got to his feet and denounced the paper. He had never read so many inaccuracies in one story. He had admitted that Stead had had an unwise relationship, but he was not a spy and there was no leakage of information. What was worse, the Home Secretary had been impressive – impressive enough for Fowler to say that the whole thing made the paper look cheap, and he was the very man who had felt so proud in the pub just two days earlier.

By nightfall Paula was in reflective mood. She had showered and changed into an evening dress ready for a dinner at Rules; the dinner would be boring and non-essential. She flicked again through the Stead file and made a decision, picked up the phone and asked for an outside line.

Mrs Stead was silent when Paula introduced herself and for a moment she thought the line had gone dead.

'Mrs Stead,' she repeated. 'I'm the Editor of the *Sunday*

*Register.* I believe you have complaints about our coverage . . .'

'Which I am making to the Press Council.'

'Would you like to make them to me?'

She would.

Twenty minutes later Paula drove into Quaker Mews. It was as if she already knew the place well through Morris's photographs. It was the sort of place that tourists thought of as quintessential London – the walls cement-painted in pastel, expensive cars on the cobbles, bay trees at the doors.

She knocked, saw an eye at the spy-hole and heard a chain being drawn back. She saw a self-assured woman holding the door open and a small boy staring down from the banisters.

'Sorry,' said Mrs Stead, tinkling the chain, 'but we've had to pull up the drawbridge. Nice timing.' She stood back to let Paula walk in. 'I've just got Sam off.' She looked her up and down. 'Is that how you dress for complaints?'

'Dinner,' Paula said. 'I've cancelled it.'

She led the way into the living-room and nodded at the little boy. 'That's Bruce. You're an object of some curiosity I'm afraid.'

In the living-room, tea-chests were stacked against the walls. They were filled with books and papers. The carpet had been rolled a few feet back from the wall exposing unvarnished boards.

'Do you have children?' Mrs Stead wanted to know.

'No.'

'No. I think I read somewhere that you said your work was your life.'

'Something like that.' She nodded at the tea-chests. 'When do you go?'

'Tomorrow. We thought we'd have difficulty in selling because a man was killed, but for some people it seems to have been an added attraction.'

'Was killed?' Paula said.

'What?'

'You said your husband was killed.'

'Did I? A slip of the tongue. Robert died of a heart attack.

137

Everyone knows that.' She motioned Paula to a seat and watched her for a moment. 'Do you answer all your complaints personally?'

'This is the first time.'

'I'm honoured. Why?'

'Because I think I've made a serious mistake.'

'That doesn't normally motivate a newspaper to apologise.'

'It motivates me.'

Again the woman studied her, trying to make up her mind. Paula waited.

'Your reporter harassed me and my children, Miss Croxley,' she said. 'Photographed me in secret. Told lies about me and my husband.'

'What lies?'

'You said he was a spy.'

'We did not. We . . .' But Mrs Stead silenced her with a dismissive wave of her hand. 'Oh, I know, I know,' she said. 'Alleged. But the whole implication of your sordid, wretched article was that the secret's got out that he was a homosexual. Do you know what it's like for the children?' She pointed to the door. 'You try and switch off the television, hide the papers, but it's impossible.' She affected a child's voice. ' "What do they mean, Mummy, he was Daddy's lover?" '

'You're saying he had no sexual relationship with Neilson?' Paula's voice was hard. Part of her wanted to comfort the woman; another part of her thought she was acting a role.

'No,' she said violently.

Paula flipped out a photograph of Andrew Osbourne from her bag.

'Why has he been coming to see you?' she asked.

The woman glanced at it, then glared at Paula, fists clenched, white-knuckled. 'You haven't come here to apologise, have you? You've come here to find out. I hate you. I hate the Press. Your lies and distortions. He's dead and you go on killing him every day. Was he this or was he that?' She seemed near to tears now, anger about to evaporate

138

into despair. 'He was their father and my husband. And he served his country, such as it now is.' She marched to the door and pulled it open, stood straight-backed. 'Will you please go,' she said.

Paula got up and Mrs Stead went out. There was something odd, but she did not know what it was. She had been thrown out of many a house in her time. Mrs Stead was well-bred. She wouldn't have stormed out of the room. She would have stood back, let her go first, seen her out in the proper way. Not run off like that. Paula went into the hall. The woman was not at the front door where she should have been. She turned and looked up the stairs and saw her beckoning. Slowly Paula climbed the stairs and followed her through a door, heard water splashing and looked in. Mrs Stead was leaning over the bath, turning both taps full on, and now Paula understood. She followed her inside and nodded. 'I don't think your husband was a spy,' she said softly. 'Or gave away secrets.'

'You believe me?' Mrs Stead said, turning, straightening up, her face obscured by steam.

'I believe the Home Secretary. It occurred to me that if there was no leak, no secrets missing, that could be because the people who took them were not Russians, or Poles, but British.' She held up the photograph of Osbourne. 'Is that why he's putting the pressure on you?'

'Wrong,' she said but there was a flicker of a smile. 'Still wrong. But getting warm.' She moved closer. 'I'm being listened to, Andrew says. It sounds ridiculous, but I'm frightened. This has been a nightmare.' She turned away and looked into the steam and her voice was no more than a whisper. 'Of course I knew about Robert's boys, although I persuaded myself they were just friends, until you put it into words.' Then she shook her head. 'No, that's not quite true. Until Neilson. That became serious. It nearly broke up our marriage and finished Bob's career. Neilson was blackmailing him. Bob told Andrew. He wanted to resign. Andrew persuaded him not to, provided he ended the

139

relationship. I was in the country with the children that Saturday. Bob rang from the airport. Neilson was threatening him, said he'd copied documents. Bob came home here . . .' It was almost enough. Her eyes closed, but Paula couldn't let her stop.

'And?'

'The left hand didn't know what the right hand was doing.'

'What?'

She shook her head. 'I can't say any more. Don't you see? Andrew hasn't been putting the pressure on me. He wants the truth to come out.'

'Will he speak to me?'

'No.' Violent again. 'You mustn't approach him. Or me again. Please. I've been asked, told not to say anything. It's absurd, but I'm frightened you see . . .' A door creaked open on the landing. '. . . they'll stop the pension.' And then she pushed Paula out, her voice almost inaudible. 'You'll get something. Please can you . . .' Her son's face peered round the door . . . 'find your own way out?'

It was time to go. Paula went, knowing there was nothing to gain by pressing the woman further. As she let herself out and walked to the car, one phrase stuck: 'You'll get something.' What did she mean? Was it a plea or a promise?

# Fifteen

In the Rolls Royce heading towards Soho, Bennet was grinning as he filled Schiff in on the background of the man they were going to meet for lunch.

'I said to Debbie: "Look. I want someone who knows the ropes, who's held office and fallen from grace, someone in trouble who needs money." And do you know what she said?'

Schiff shrugged a 'don't know' at him.

' "That shouldn't be too difficult," she said in that tinkling little voice of hers.' Bennet's grin widened. 'Good girl, that Debbie.'

'Worth her wages,' said Schiff, which was the highest compliment he paid anyone.

'Yep. Within a couple of hours she had found Somers for me. Jeremy Somers, ex-Home Secretary. He has wife problems, tax problems and the Prime Minister hates him. But he's an old friend of the Secretary of State.'

The car stopped outside a restaurant and Schiff looked out.

'And he likes Chinese food,' he suggested.

'So Debbie says.'

Somers was late. He came into the restaurant noisily, first-naming the waiters, accepting their nods of greeting with a fluttering hand, a big man gone to fat. The introductions were made, the orders given, and, immediately, as always, Bennet came straight to the point. Somers listened without

141

interruption, then sipped wine in silence for a moment before replying.

'What you're offering me,' he said in a Tory drawl, his eyes half closed, 'is more than I got as a Cabinet minister.' He smiled. 'For advice?'

'The Government doesn't appreciate your talents as we do,' Schiff said.

'Evidently.' He waved to a group at a far table, a limp-handed gesture. It reminded Bennet of royalty in a coach. 'I'll think about it,' he said.

'I'm afraid we need an answer now,' Bennet said. 'There is something specific. We're planning to buy the *Mercury* and there's another bidder from outside the industry, so he's unlikely to be stopped by the Monopolies Commission.'

'And you will be,' Somers said.

'Yes. And we can't afford to be held up for six months. A year.'

Somers lazily chewed this over and delicately sipped wine. 'And what do you expect me to do about it?' he said at last.

Schiff was straight in. 'Help us with our case.'

'What case?'

Bennet took over. 'The one you're going to find.'

'I see.' Somers smiled, laid down his knife and fork, and clasped his hands like a preacher.

'I only own the *Register*,' Bennet said.

'Fair Trading Act,' Somers said. 'Goes by combined circulations, not number of papers.'

'It would be ridiculous to refer it,' Bennet said.

'You want me to pull a string?'

Schiff held up his hand. 'Or two,' he said, wiggling his fingers.

'I see why the fee is so high,' Somers said, thoughtful again. He filled up his wine glass, but did not pass the bottle round. 'Mr Bennet, I've been an MP for twenty years, held office for five . . .'

Here we go, thought Schiff, the bloody British sounding off again, the pompous assholes.

142

'. . . you people think you can buy this Great House? Or me? Do you think I'm that much in need of money?'

Bennet said nothing, just gazed at him, waiting for him to answer himself. He had made his protest, now he would talk sense.

'You have an inflated idea of what a backbencher can do,' Somers said.

'You're close to the Secretary of State for Industry,' Bennet offered.

'George?' He laughed. 'I can't just go to him and say "Please George." You can't buy him.'

'You can buy everybody, Mr Somers.'

'Rubbish. We're not as corrupt as the States. Yet.' He looked at Schiff. 'Things aren't like that here.'

'How does it work then?' Schiff asked, all innocence, wanting to know.

Somers looked from one to the other, then clasped his fingers again. Another fuckin' speech coming up, Schiff reckoned.

'Mr Bennet,' Somers said. 'I won't deny I need money so badly I would even accept it from you. But I'm sorry. You may have a case, but at present you won't even get the benefit of the doubt. We're running up to an election. Everything must be whiter than white. At the moment George would refer a market-stall owner to the Monopolies Commission.'

Bennet shrugged. 'I've got to have that paper,' he said loudly so that heads turned. He lowered his voice. 'My whole future, the whole future of my UK base depends on it.'

Somers patted his arm. 'There's nothing I, or anyone else, can do to help you, Mr Bennet.'

Schiff looked at them both, wiped his mouth with his napkin and smiled. 'As you say, John, heads I win, tails I lose.' He turned to Somers. 'This fish is excellent.'

No one knew who brought the envelope. The man on the front desk found it in the mail and could not put a face to anyone who might have slipped it amongst the letters and packages. Fowler was the first to read it and within five minutes Paula had called Stone, Merton and the Defence Correspondent, Gerry Carlton, to her office. She held it in front of her as the three men settled themselves, then handed it to Carlton.

'This was written by a civil servant in the Ministry of Defence,' she said. 'It's the draft reply to the parliamentary question on Stead.'

'It's innocuous,' Merton added. 'The covering letter is the giveaway.'

Greene read aloud: ' "... also relevant is the minute of the Ministerial Group on Security, May 5, but as this minute is highly classified, there is no need to admit there was a security operation in progress at the time of Stead's death." '

Stone snapped his fingers. 'There it is,' he said. 'Black and white. They were raiding his house, looking for evidence.'

Paula nodded, thinking back to the previous evening. 'You'll get something,' Mrs Stead had said.

'Well,' Carlton drawled, thinking on his feet. 'It fits with what Mrs Stead told you. The Defence Ministry has its own police, its own security. Stead would have what's called his reporting officer. He confesses to him about Neilson, there's no leak, it's a peccadillo. Now, either MI5 don't believe them or perhaps they don't even know.'

'And they do what we did,' Merton said. 'Jump to conclusions.'

Carlton nodded. 'Neilson's whole description smells of an illegal MI5 burglary going terribly wrong. He thought the man coming out of the house was Stead for a moment. MI5 would be very careful. One person dressed like Stead would enter so that neighbours would be fooled. He would use duplicate keys. His driver would remain in radio contact with another man following Stead. I can only imagine that when Stead and Neilson went through passport control, this man thought they'd boarded. Then when Stead arrived . . ' He left the sentence hanging for a moment, then looked at Paula.

'They'll throw everything at you to try and stop you publishing.'

'They won't know until it's too late,' she said and looked from one face to another. 'Who's seen this? The four of us. No one else need know.'

'Toby will have to know,' Stone said.

'He's going on holiday. I don't want to bother him.'

'Bennet?' Merton suggested.

'It's nothing to do with him. It's an editorial decision.'

Merton began pacing. 'It's a criminal offence. We're breaking the Official Secrets Act. Someone's got to play devil's advocate.'

'I'll see the lawyers,' Paula said. 'It might be better for Bennet if he doesn't know . . .' Then she was interrupted by Merton slapping his forehead. 'I'm an idiot,' he said. 'I'm getting too excited. Jim saw it.'

'Fowler?' Paula asked.

'He picked it out. I told him to keep quiet.'

'That means he'll only whisper it,' Stone said.

Paula yanked the door open. 'Get him in here, Alan,' she said.

A moment later, they were five.

'My lips are sealed,' Fowler said, but Paula was looking at him suspiciously. The man had never been known to keep a secret. It was one of the reasons he would always be someone's deputy.

'After all, Jim,' Merton said, 'you don't want to be involved in a criminal activity.'

Fowler stiffened. 'It's the Editor they go for,' he said.

'You received it,' Merton said.

And Paula spelled it out for him – something he should have known by now. 'The Official Secrets Act is a crazy catch-all. You're guilty if you send classified information to unauthorised people. You're guilty if you receive it and stay quiet. Look at what they tried to do to Ponting.'

'What happens when we publish?' Fowler asked.

'There'll be such a bloody outcry they won't dare touch us,'

145

she said, then leant forward, elbows on her desk, working out a strategy. 'I'll alter the schedule so Bill Wakely will be Night Editor. We can trust him. And I don't want anything set until the last possible moment.'

She shooed them out like geese and, when she was alone, she winked at each of the portraits in turn, feeling more alive than she had for six months.

For six hours throughout the afternoon and evening, John Bennet had paced his room in the Grosvenor House Hotel, searching for a solution and trying to keep an almost unknown emotion at bay. He was facing despair for the first time in years; his mind kept conjuring up unwanted images – a stag at bay, the hounds snapping at its heels; a ship deserted by rats – and he had to force himself to concentrate and work on the problem. There *had* to be a solution. There always had been. Until now.

Then, at nine, the phone rang. It was Somers wanting to see him. Soonest, the man said. Where? The Reform Club. Bennet replaced the receiver and whooped with delight, causing Debbie to jump, startled, and ask what was wrong. The answer was nothing. He hoped. Why would Somers call unless he had come up with something? He called for his car, went into the bathroom to wash and change and, when he looked in the mirror, there were no longer any cornered stags or scampering rats. He tingled again with pleasant apprehension.

Half an hour later he was walking around the library in the club, with Somers at his elbow. They were looking at the portraits and Bennet did not push the man, permitted him his moment of small talk. There were proprieties to be observed. In England, it was bad manners to come straight to the point.

They stopped at the portrait of Glenross, and Bennet looked up at it. The last time he saw it was when Ormsby stormed out of the office. It had been a nice touch, he thought, to donate it to the club.

146

'So you know this place?' Somers drawled.

'I used to see Glenross here.'

'When you bought the *Register*?'

'Yes.'

'I hope that's an auspicious sign. For your purchase of the *Daily Mercury*.'

Bennet glanced at him, saw the slight smile quivering the thin lips. 'You said it was impossible . . .'

'So it is, so it is.' Somers saw a waiter passing and raised a hand. 'But it might be one of those impossibles that takes a little longer.' He smiled and indicated a table. 'Shall we?'

The man would not be hurried and Bennet fought to contain his impatience. Somers rambled for a while about the old days, staring into his brandy glass, telling parliamentary anecdotes. All very interesting, Bennet thought, for an after-dinner conversation, but not now. As Somers talked, Bennet wondered who he had been in touch with that afternoon, and what devious little plan had been hatched in some smoke-filled drawing-room somewhere. And then at last he came to the point.

'Bingo, Mr Bennet.'

'Huh?'

'That's the winning line. Under the Act, section fifty-eight, sub-section three, if the Secretary of State is satisfied the *Daily Mercury* is not a going concern, he may not refer it to the Monopolies Commission.'

Bennet did not understand. 'But it *is* profitable,' he said. 'Just.'

'Then make it unprofitable. Get them to increase the bingo prizes by half a million or so, which could be . . . ah, adjusted in the price you pay.'

Bennet nodded and began to smile, then remembered something Somers had just said. 'The Secretary *may* not refer it,' he said. 'There's no guarantee?'

'Of course not.' He paused, sipped brandy and stared for a moment at the ceiling. Bennet tapped his fingers. The man was enjoying himself, stretching out his proposal for all it was

147

worth. 'Tell you what might help,' he said chirpily.

Bennet waited.

'The Stead stories in your paper have been a little embarrassing to the government. This is nothing to do with the Secretary of State's decision . . .'

'Of course not,' Bennet said. Now all was revealed. The price was there before him.

'We would merely be creating a favourable climate for it,' Somers said.

'I understand.'

Somers raised his glass. Bennet clinked it with his. 'That was last week's story,' Bennet said. 'Don't worry. Stead is dead.'

'Then long live the *Mercury*,' Somers said.

148

# Sixteen

Bill Sutcliffe should have been a happy man. The big City story was literally on his doorstep. Outside, the opposition waited, frustrated and impotent. He had the whole damn story to himself, but the problem was that the man at the centre of it was his proprietor, and he did not know how to handle it. He stood in his Editor's office looking gloomily at the lunchtime edition of the *Standard* and the headline: *Bennet Bids For Mercury*.

He did not know what to do. He could not afford to annoy Bennet. He had, after all, a mortgage and an ex-wife to support. Plus, when he asked his Editor how he should approach it, he was snapped at.

'I don't know,' Paula said. 'You're the City Editor. You tell me.'

'Well, the Secretary ought to refer the bid to the Monopolies Commission . . .'

'Then say so.'

Sutcliffe sighed and turned to go.

'Everyone else will,' she said to his back. 'We'd only look sycophantic if we ignored it. Treat him like any other proprietor. He'll have to fire me before he fires you.'

He went reluctantly and Paula called for her secretary and began rifling through a pile of invitations. 'Right,' she muttered. 'Who else wants to corrupt us?'

Angela took the pile from her. 'Sir John Walsham,' she read, 'Junior Minister for . . .'

'Regret,' said Paula.

'Annual Dinner of the Worshipful Company of Ironmongers.'

'Give that to Toby.'

'The Home Secretary.'

Paula took the card. 'Reception.' She frowned. 'What does he want to invite me for after all the nasty things I've said about him?'

'So you'll be nicer,' said Angela.

'No doubt,' she said. 'Accept. And while I remember, make an appointment with the lawyer. Not the duty man. I want Jimmie Chapel.'

She went to the window and looked into the street. From her office she could see the back door of the Feathers. The door was open. Two men were going in for an early one – Jim Fowler and Toby Greene. In her imagination, they looked like conspirators. They should be wearing togas, she thought, the better to hide their stabbing knives. Then she put away her imagination and went back to work . . .

It was what was known as holiday-ale time, which meant that Greene was buying.

Fowler raised his glass to him. 'Lucky bugger,' he said. 'Two weeks away from this dump. How do you feel?'

'Nervous. Remember the first rule of Fleet Street. Never go on holiday.'

Fowler nodded. 'I know the feeling. Before Beaverbrook collapsed I remember Piranha Teeth went skiing and Max Aitken phoned him and . . .'

'. . . told him not to hurry back.' Greene nodded. It was an ancient tale. What he was more interested in was the present and the future. 'What's going on, Jim?' he asked.

'I'm always the last to know.'

'Come off it,' he said, scoffing. 'You see more than anyone from the top of the fence. Why has Bill Wakely been switched to Night Editor on Saturday?'

'You do the rota,' Fowler said.

'She's changed it. She's got something up her sleeve. You

think she's on top, Jim, but she's flying too near the sun.' He took out a pen and scribbled on a beer mat. 'If her wings start to melt, phone this number.'

Fowler took it and frowned. 'I thought you were going to Italy.'

'Devon's nearer,' Greene said.


Across the road and three floors above, Debbie Cartwright fixed her professional smile and marched unannounced into the Editor's office. She thought she'd need it. She was going to have to be terribly diplomatic.

'I'm awfully sorry to trouble you, Paula,' she said sweetly. 'You've received an invitation from the Home Secretary.'

'Yes.'

'It was sent to you by mistake.'

'Really?' Paula's smile matched that of the younger woman. 'How do you know that?'

'It was meant for Mr Bennet.'

'All press invitations go to the Editor,' Paula said, still smiling.

'This isn't a press reception,' Debbie insisted. 'It's one for various distinguished people.'

'And I'm not distinguished?'

Debbie blushed. She'd blundered, and stammered an apology.

'Well, I'm awfully sorry, Debbie,' Paula said briskly. 'I've already accepted.'

'Angela hasn't sent it,' she said, smiling again. She'd asked on the way in.

'I telephoned,' Paula said.

'You could always be ill.'

Paula had had enough. She had work to do. A moment sparring with Bennet's pretty young girl was pleasant enough but it had gone on too long. 'Debbie, if *The Times* and the *Telegraph* are going to be there, I certainly am. If Mr Bennet is short of a free drink, there's always the Worshipful Company of Ironmongers.'

Debbie was dismissed. On her way out, she reckoned that her boss was going to be angry with her. She would just have to get him another invitation, and idly wondered what on earth the ironmongers found to worship in this day and age . . .

For the reception Paula chose black silk. Alan Merton whistled when he saw her. 'High society,' he said. 'Why aren't you going with Bennet?'

'I shall have enough of him there,' she said.

'OK, then may I offer you a lift?'

She accepted and he guided her down the stairs to the car-park, quietly fantasising, thinking how nice it would be if it were he who were actually going to the reception and not just acting as chauffeur.

'Time you got a new car,' she said as he opened the door of the old Renault.

'On what they pay me?'

He drove in silence for a while, vaguely aware that she was studying him. Then she leant across and asked, 'How would you feel about being Deputy Editor?'

'We already have a Deputy Editor.'

'You practically do the job now.'

He shook his head. 'Bennet won't have it. He wants to keep playing you off against one another.'

She was silent for a moment, then she said softly, 'He told me we should co-operate, and I believed him. I actually tried. How bloody naïve I was six months ago. It feels like six years!'

Round Trafalgar Square they were silent and it wasn't until Merton swung the car into Pall Mall and saw the police and the line of limousines, that he spoke. 'Suppose I don't want the job?'

'You will.' She looked out and saw Bennet getting out of the Rolls. She waved but he ignored her. 'Alan,' she said, 'I'm going to do what I should have done a long time ago.'

And she was out and the cameras were raised and someone in uniform was welcoming her.

She had thought she would be nervous, but she felt at ease, mingling with others she knew before being called into the main reception room. She felt as though she were at an airport waiting for her flight to be called and, as she joined in the small talk, she thought back to her meeting that afternoon with Chapel. He'd told her the legal position. Publish and she was open to prosecution, a fine or maybe prison, and she had wondered aloud in front of him how high the lie about Stead's death had gone and how much the Home Secretary knew.

'Go easy.' Bennet was at her shoulder, smiling at her, but there was no warmth in his tone.

'Go easy?' she said, fluttering her eyelashes at him.

'Behave yourself. Remember I'm buying the *Mercury*. At least I *hope* I'm buying the *Mercury*.'

They were moving now towards the front of the line. Ahead they could see the Home Secretary in the main reception room shaking hands with someone.

'You mean they won't sell it to you if I get too many order marks?' Paula whispered.

'Paula, please. I know this mood of yours.'

'Do you?' He did not. He thought he did but he was way off beam. He was looking ahead now, watching as they got to the head of the line, then he leant into her shoulder and whispered, 'These shits could crucify me.'

'How?'

'Just steer clear of the heavy crap. Defence secrets. Spies.' They had reached the Master of Ceremonies now, but Bennet did not notice. 'This is a social occasion . . .'

'Tell the man your name,' Paula said.

'What?'

'Your name.'

'Oh,' he smiled at the man. 'Bennet.'

The man turned. The Home Secretary waited three paces away.

'MR AND MRS BENNET!'

Bennet blinked. Paula snorted with suppressed laughter,

153

then the Home Secretary smiled. 'I think that's not quite right,' he said.

Bennet recovered quickly, the dazzling smile on full beam now. 'We have a close relationship, Home Secretary, but not that close.'

'You've put the old *Register* back on its feet,' the Home Secretary said, then turned to Paula. 'Miss Croxley, hello. I may not agree with everything you say, but you say it very well.'

Briefly, Paula's composure left her. She felt like a child in front of the headmaster, and she could only stammer a couple of 'thank you's', while the Master of Ceremonies made the next announcement and they were left again to mingle.

It was champagne and canapés. Paula remembered the ex-Prime Minister who had presented her with her award and that lovely story of the beer and sandwiches meetings, when the PM had introduced Herr Willy Brandt to a journalist called Worsthorne and Brandt had said *'gesundheit'*. She smiled at the memory, an apocryphal story no doubt, then looked up to see the Home Secretary's group in the far corner, and an old man, fat and balding, winking at her.

Bennet was talking to her, something about her plugging into a few power points or some such nonsense, then he, too, caught the little man winking.

'Lord Bayswater,' he said, lowering his voice. 'He's got his eye on you. He's a corrupt old lech but he has the ear of the PM. You waggle your tits at him while I nobble the Secretary of State.' Bennet grinned at her as he saw the little man come towards them. 'What a team,' he said, made the introductions and excused himself.

Bayswater waited until he had gone, then turned to Paula, red-cheeked, twinkling eyes. 'Giving you instructions was he?'

'Oh, he wouldn't dare do that.'

'You run the show, do you?'

'Of course.'

He nodded. 'I used to read you when you were a respectable journalist.' The smile diluted the insult and Paula smiled back. 'I expect you say that because I wrote only foreign stories.'

The man shrugged, his smile dying. 'Seriously, the dear old *Register* really does bear his hallmark,' he said.

'And what's that?'

Bayswater turned, looked at Bennet who was listening intently to a group in the corner, then turned back to Paula and spoke as if he were an old friend. 'To put it at its politest,' he paused, 'sensational fantasy masquerading as truth. But fortunately he does seem to be absorbing some of the values of this country.'

'Does he?'

Bayswater raised a finger to his lips and grinned like a little boy caught smoking in the lavatories. 'Better not say any more.' He nodded at his glass. 'Too many bubbles.' He looked at her. She seemed stern. 'Oh, come on,' he said, striving for levity. 'He's a rogue. Out for what he can get.'

She pulled away from him. 'He's not,' she said loudly, surprising herself. Maybe it was the lecherous way he put it. Maybe it was because he was a civilian, one of those who did not know what newspapers were like, and what their problems were – one of those smug little men who criticised. It was the easiest thing in the world to criticise from the sidelines. 'That's just the impression he gives,' she continued. 'And the one you like to have.'

She was too loud. The group around the Home Secretary looked round, but she did not care. 'He's a good publisher. He knows every inch of the business. He's full of ideas. He's rescued the paper with his own money and if there's any fantasy in it, that's my responsibility.'

'Stead for instance?' Bayswater offered.

'Stead for instance,' Paula agreed.

The group around the Home Secretary was intent on them now, but trying not to make their attention seem obvious.

'If there's no Philby this week,' Bayswater prompted, 'let's invent one.'

155

'All right,' Paula agreed. 'We got it wrong.'

'And *how*, my dear.'

*My dear.* The patronising little shit. 'But we'll get it right.'

A voice at her shoulder made her twitch, startled. 'You mean there are more fantasies to come?' It was the Home Secretary. She had been unaware of his interest. Now the group was all around her, but this time she did not stammer. 'Realities, Home Secretary.'

'That sounds mysterious,' he said with a smile.

Then Bennet was pushing his way towards her. In his haste to get to her, he brushed past Bayswater, knocking his elbow, spilling champagne over Paula's dress and spraying apologies in all directions. 'I'm sorry, Lord Bayswater. I'm sorry, Paula. That was entirely my fault.' Then he was guiding her out, smiling, making amends, towards the ante-room . . .

It took her ten minutes to mop up and come out of the bathroom.

'All right?' Bennet asked. He was alone, pacing, the door to the reception room closed.

'You did that deliberately,' she said and tried to move past him.

'You can't go back in there,' he said and grabbed her arm.

'I most certainly can.'

'Do you know what you look like?'

They were almost spitting at one another, like cats before a fight.

'What are you plotting?' Paula asked.

'What?' Bennet asked.

'Something Bayswater said. You're learning the rules, he said. He said you . . .' But he snapped at her, holding her arm tight. 'You're paranoid, Paula. Go home. Take my car.'

She snatched her arm away, stepped clear of him and blazed, 'If you're going back in, so am I.'

He swore at her as the door opened and people spilled out, smiling at them. They smiled back and, when he looked at her again, she was smiling sweetly at him as if they were the best of friends – almost as if they were Mr and Mrs Bennet.

'Could you get my coat, please?' Paula said. With everyone around him, he had no choice . . .

In the Rolls, the fight was brief and violent.

'I'm wet through,' she snapped at him.

'I told you not to raise the subject.'

'I,' she said, tapping her chest, 'did not raise it.'

'You were asking the Home Secretary . . .'

'I'm not *that* bloody tactless. I was setting up an interview. You ruined it.'

'And you nearly ruined my paper, my whole set-up here.'

'How? How do I know what to say if you don't tell me what's going on?'

He shrugged, too angry to continue, and, for the rest of the journey, they sat in simmering silence, until the chauffeur's voice gurgled through the intercom, 'This block, madam?'

'By the rubbish bags. Thank you.'

The car stopped. She got out, turned to him and surprised him. 'Will you come up? I have something to say.'

He glanced at his watch, nodded, got out and told the chauffeur to drive on. He would get a taxi later.

Inside, Paula made for the kitchen and picked up the kettle. Briefly he thought she was going to hit him with it, then she smiled. 'I was actually defending you,' she said.

'I don't need defending, thanks.'

'That's the trouble.'

But she had made the first peace move and there was nothing for him to do but respond. 'I've never had an executive talk to me like that.'

'That's the trouble,' she said again.

She was filling the kettle as he approached. 'What's wrong?' he asked. 'Are you resigning?'

She turned, shocked by the question. The kettle twisted in her hand, the water hit the spout and sprayed them both and she started laughing, the tension eased by the sight of him backing away, grabbing at a roll of kitchen tissue hanging from the wall.

'I'm sorry,' she said. 'Not my night . . .'

He yanked at the tissue, pulled the spindle off the wall, sending the roll looping in the air, causing her to break into hysterical laughter, and the angrier he became, the more she laughed.

'If you've got something to say,' he said, biting off each syllable as if it were painful to talk, 'then say it.'

'Let me change,' she said, holding up her hands in surrender, fighting to stop the laughter, to be serious in front of him. 'No. I'm not resigning. No. On the contrary. Are you disappointed?'

'I put up with you because . . .'

'. . . because you've sold me to a million readers. The gimmick rebounds.'

Bennet finished mopping his jacket and pointed an accusing finger at her. 'You're not the paper, Paula. If I wanted to get rid of you, I'd get rid of you.'

'And don't you want to? After tonight?'

'It won't take much more.'

She battered the kettle on the sink, glared at him and surprised him again. 'Oh . . . why don't you have a drink?'

'Red wine or coffee?'

'Bourbon.' She pointed to a cluster of bottles on a shelf.

'That's my bourbon,' he said.

She flipped a hand towards the fridge. 'Ice? Lemon?' Then she pushed past him. 'I'm going to get out of this dishcloth. Can you do one for me, please.'

It took him a couple of minutes to find everything and to crush the ice. He poured two drinks, tucked the bottle under his arm and went into the living-room. It was the same as before. A mess, a clutter – as if a grenade of stationery had exploded. Paula, wearing a bathrobe, came out of the bathroom. She switched on a table-lamp and took her drink. 'I'm moving,' she said.

'Where?'

'Somewhere more appropriate. I stayed here because I didn't know if I would last in the job.'

'And now you think you will?'

'Oh yes.' She smiled and nodded. 'It's not that I've realised how good I am, but just how bloody mediocre most other people in high places are.' She pointed her glass towards her typewriter and the stack of A4 paper, virgin white. 'I used to think that what I did was important, but I've realised that words without power are worse than useless. It's the words that are left out that are important. Or what's between the words.' She gulped her drink. 'Secrets.' He topped up her glass as she continued. 'Look at them all swarming around the Home Secretary tonight, like insects under a stone. I want to lift the stone and watch some of those fat, white creatures scuttle for cover.'

She raised her glass, said, 'Cheers', and waited for his reaction.

'What secrets are we talking about?' he asked.

She shrugged. 'I was generalising.'

'You said to Bayswater that there was more on Stead.'

'I just wanted to see how he would react. That's all.'

'If there's more, I'd like to know.'

She nodded in agreement, looked down in surprise. Her glass was empty again. She had been drinking like there was Prohibition coming. 'Well,' she said, 'all that noble sentiment is why I intend to stay on the paper.'

'And what about me?'

She looked at him for a moment, then fluttered her fingers across his chest. 'I'm going to treat you like you treat me.'

'And how is that?'

In reply she took the bottle from him and tilted it towards his glass, then began to tremble, once more on the edge of laughter.

'What is it?' he asked, genuinely puzzled.

She shook her head. 'I can't do it.'

'What?'

'The trouble is, you haven't much sense of humour.' She

159

put her hand to her mouth as the laughter began to overtake her.

'I haven't *your* sense of humour,' he said.

'I was going to . . .' She rocked with suppressed laughter and he grabbed the glass from her as the bourbon dribbled over the rim. First champagne, then water, now bourbon, he thought . . . then she was laughing at him, letting it out. 'I was going to seduce you,' she said. 'To have you in my power. Oh, God,' she giggled, 'but I don't have your dedication, your high seriousness, your single-minded . . .' She searched for the word, gave up and posed, a caricature of a seductress, her arms tight against her breasts, hands caressing her thighs. 'I was going to seduce you, then I couldn't make up my mind whether you would be in my power if I let you have me . . . if I seduced you or . . .' She was gabbling and he silenced her by kissing her, then she pushed away from him, still trembling with laughter. 'Oh, God, oh, no, look, I think this would be a dreadful mistake . . .' He kissed her again. '. . . It could ruin a good working relationship,' she said. 'This isn't what I intended, well, the way I intended.' He was moving towards her again and suddenly she made up her mind. 'Oh, what the hell. Everybody thinks we're doing it. Let's get it over with.'

# Seventeen

It had been a long time and she had forgotten how much she had missed it, and, now that it was over, she felt a curious mix of relief and apprehension – whatever happened, things had changed irrevocably. She remembered the cover of *Private Eye*. There was a phrase for it somewhere. Lazily she searched for it – *self-fulfilling prophecy*, that was it. Maybe it had been a mistake, but as she'd said an hour earlier, what the hell; she'd made her bed and now she was lying in it. The thought made her chuckle, then she opened her eyes.

'I don't understand anything,' she muttered. She didn't understand how this had happened and who had seduced whom.

'Here, as even Walter would say,' he murmured, 'you don't have to.'

'Where is he? Under the bed?'

'Maybe. He thinks he's going to break me.'

'How?'

In the darkness she could not make out his expression. 'I was generalising,' he said.

She stuck out her tongue at him, then he was on her again, heavy against her, and she could see him now. He was grinning – an evil grin, pretending to be threatening. 'What have you found out about Stead, you bitch?' At least, she thought he was pretending, hoped he was pretending. She played the same game. 'What was Bayswater on about?'

He laughed and lay back. 'We're two of a kind,' she said.

'I'm afraid so.'

'Only you've had more practice.'

'A little.'

'Much more.'

'You're catching up.' He leant on an elbow and looked down at her. 'You're planning to run something. You've changed the rota.' She pouted at him, all injured innocence. 'Come on,' he said. 'I'll camp in the machine-room.'

Maybe he would, she thought. She wouldn't put it past him. And besides, he had a right to know. He was, after all, the bloody proprietor.

'I was going to tell you,' she said quietly. 'I was waiting for the right moment.'

'When the first edition was off the press?' he suggested.

She shook her head. 'On the streets.' Like she said, *what the hell?* 'We have a confidential Cabinet document . . .'

She awoke full of energy, despite the slight hangover. Sex was good for her – always had been. He had left a note propped against the bourbon bottle: *Thanks*. That was all and it was enough. It was a warm morning. The traffic was light. The conference was full of ideas and, in two days' time, she was going to produce a newspaper which would make the country blink.

Then two men were ushered into her office and everything changed. Two men in suits, one carrying a neatly folded overcoat over his arm, hard-looking men, one in his fifties, she reckoned, the one with the coat ten years younger, neither one looking as if they had ever known how to smile.

'Sorry to disturb you like this, madam,' said the older one, introducing himself as Chief Inspector Phillips, Ministry of Defence Police, and Inspector Fisher, and as soon as she heard the names, she added two and two and made four, and felt more angry and betrayed and foolish than she had ever known.

Five minutes later she stormed unannounced into Bennet's office. He was seated at his desk, Schiff looking over his shoulder at a contract.

'I want to see you now,' she said to Bennet. 'And I want to see you alone, please.'

Bennet looked at her, then at Schiff. Schiff nodded and made for the door. He smiled at Paula but she ignored him. 'Walter,' Bennet said as the little man went out. 'Couldn't we deal with that clause by a side letter?'

'Sure.' And he went out, leaving them together. She glared at him, fought for self-control and lost, and her voice broke as she told him, 'I've had the police here. That document. In my office. Two of them. They've thrown the Official Secrets Act at me.'

'Calm down,' he said, but there was no chance.

'It's not just that they know, but you told them.'

'*I* told them?'

'Of course you did.'

'Don't be stupid. Why . . .'

'I know,' she shouted, all attempts at restraint gone now. 'I know you. It's too much of a coincidence . . .'

'You can't believe that,' he interrupted. 'You know the last place you can keep a secret is in a newspaper office.' He shook his head, affecting disbelief. 'After all I've done on Stead, the way I've supported you, backed you. Do you think I don't want to expose the lying shits?' He spread his hands. 'That you can think I . . . ? After last night.'

And she believed him. And she knew why she believed him. It was cliché time again. She believed him because she wanted to believe him. She even apologised and he came up to her and placed his hands on her shoulders. 'Come on,' he said softly. 'It's a pity they've got it but . . .'

'They haven't,' she said.

'Huh?'

'No. You don't think I'd give them it, do you? I didn't even admit to having it.'

He turned away from her, frowning. 'Did they search . . .?'

'No. They were there to put the frighteners on me, threaten me with prosecution if I published.'

'It's a criminal offence.'

She cursed softly and he turned to look at her. She had regained her composure now. 'Have you seen the writs in my office?' she said. 'There are hundreds of unauthorised documents in Fleet Street.'

'Not as hot as this one.'

Briefly she wondered why he was being cautious. It didn't go with his reputation. 'The fine would be paid off in extra circulation,' she said.

'It might mean prison.'

'So? I'll write a column from my cell.' Something was wrong, she thought. He was supposed to be the hard man. By reputation he should have been the one encouraging her to go to prison for the sake of selling more papers. 'You were saying you wanted to get rid of the bastards,' she said.

'Yes.'

'You'll back me?'

'Yes.'

Good, she thought and turned to go, but he was still talking. 'Yes, of course I'll back you. One hundred per cent.' But there was something wrong with his tone. There was a 'but' coming. She could feel it. 'But we've got to be realistic,' he said.

She sighed and stopped at the door, feeling the tears begin to cloud her vision and hating herself for her naïvety.

'Realistic,' she said.

'Listen . . .'

'So it was you.' She turned and leant back against the door. 'Will you listen?'

'You've done some kind of a deal. You . . .'

He strode three paces towards her, gripped her shoulders and glared at her. 'If you think that, we might as well quit. If we print this story, the Government will refer our bid for the *Mercury* to the Monopolies Commission.'

She pushed him off. 'I was right,' she roared at him. 'You've done a deal.'

'I have not,' he yelled back. 'Do you think any government would be stupid enough to do such a thing? I'll spell it out for you. There's a case to be made for referring the *Mercury*. There's a case to be made for not referring it. If we publish, which case do you think they will choose?' He gave her no time to consider an answer. 'If we lose the *Mercury*, then a new printing plant for the *Register* is uneconomic. The *Register* can't go on without new plant. I will pull out.' He stepped back a pace and she sagged against the door. His tone changed. He was softer again. He'd made his point and he could see the signs of defeat in her face. 'I know what you feel, Paula, I know. Hell, this story might be huge. Do you think I don't want to print it?' She shrugged, as if she no longer cared. 'But not at the price of committing suicide . . .' And before he had reached the end of the sentence, she was out and heading for the lift, thinking that only a few minutes ago she had been a bundle of enthusiasm and now she felt like heading for the nearest tall building . . .

Ten minutes later, in the flat in the Grosvenor House Hotel, Walter Schiff was nodding approval into the phone.

'So, how did you do it?' he asked.

'She's a sensible woman,' Bennet replied.

'Sensible? You told her about the deal?'

'Don't be stupid. She'd have it all round Fleet Street.'

Schiff nodded as Bennet asked him how the *Mercury* deal was progressing. 'Minor clauses,' he said. 'Nothing serious.'

'Good.' Bennet sounded happy. 'Let's forget our differences, Walter,' he said. 'I'm standing here looking out the window. All I can see down there are crazy faces. Tension, stress, ulcers, heart disease – and what for?'

Schiff shrugged.

'When all this is over,' Bennet continued, 'I'm going to take a holiday.'

Holiday? Schiff thought. What was a holiday? 'With me?' he squeaked and Bennet's laughter crackled through the receiver.

'No, not with you, Walter, not with you, you old bastard.'

And he hung up. Schiff looked into the receiver for a

moment and smiled. Bennet sounded as happy as he had ever been and Walter Schiff, gently replacing the receiver, hoped the mood would last.

She had spent all day thinking about it and trying not to think about herself. She had to be objective. Women were supposed to be emotional, weren't they? The old condemnation. They could go only so far and then their emotions took over and blinded their judgment. How often had she heard that one in the bars and at the dinner-tables? Maybe all her adult life, was the answer. And now, thinking about the problem, she kept having to force the idea of betrayal out of her mind – the possibility that she had been used and abused. It was not important. What was important was to do the right thing.

She had tried calling him, but Debbie had become an expert bodyguard over the past six months. All day he had been unavailable, but now it was close to midnight and the bodyguard would have gone home.

No one took any notice of her as she passed reception in the hotel and made for the lift. Maybe he would have a woman with him. A small part of her hoped so. She would enjoy bursting in on them – after last night – but he was awake, and alone, dressed formally. She could see a dinner-jacket on the chair. He even tried to kiss her as she walked in and she had to brush him off.

'I haven't come for that,' she said flatly, then shook her head. 'I'm sorry.'

'What's wrong?'

'I've got to publish the story.' She saw him making for the cocktail cabinet. 'I don't want a drink,' she said.

He stopped and smiled at her. 'You haven't got to do anything,' he said.

'I have. If I didn't, I wouldn't feel I had any integrity left.' She saw the look of bewilderment on his face, as if he did not know what the word meant. 'I know it sounds pompous,' she continued, then checked herself, angry at the way she was putting her point. 'Why the hell should I apologise? What sort of a society do we live in when you have to apologise for integrity?'

'Ego,' he answered.

'What?'

'Ego. Integrity! You want to be the person who exposed the cover-up, just as I want to be the one who pulled off the *Mercury* deal.'

It wasn't a good enough answer. 'I don't care what you call it,' she said and turned to go, but he stopped her. 'Paula,' he said, running between her and the door, 'I haven't told you everything. It's not just the paper that will be finished. I will. The American shareholders are going for me – organised by Walter, who unfortunately hasn't any of your integrity or your loyalty. If the UK operation fails, then . . .' He attempted a lost look, that of a defeated man, but she wasn't buying.

'I don't believe you,' she said.

For a moment he glared at her and she knew she should have felt frightened but she no longer cared. It was just a moment, then he regained control, went to his desk and pulled out a letter with an airmail border and the stamp of Pacific International. She read it slowly. OK, she thought, this time you're not being devious. The Americans were indeed after his blood and maybe they would get it.

She folded it neatly and handed it back. 'I'm sorry,' she said, 'but that's your problem. Mine is to publish the story.'

He woke her with a phone-call early next morning and there was no attempt at conciliation. It was as if they were strangers – the boss and the employee – just a few seconds of stacatto conversation.

'I want that document,' he said.

'I'm sorry.'

'You are not to publish anything on Stead without my prior approval.'

'I decide what is published.'

'Think it over. You've got an hour.'

'I don't need an hour. I don't need a second.'

'Then, Paula, I'm sorry. Very sorry. I shall have to accept your resignation.'

'I'm not giving it.'

'You will.'

She hung up, more determined than ever to publish and be damned and strangely grateful to him for his attitude, because now there were no doubts. He had shown himself in his true colours – the wolf in wolf's clothing. Now there was no need to be assaulted by her emotions. All she had to do now was her job.

As she reached her office, she was aware of Angela's stricken face, her stammering condolences and, for a moment, she was perplexed. Then she saw the figure behind the frosted glass – a slim, elegant figure, someone who should have been on holiday in Italy. She threw the door open and strode into her office. Toby Greene was running the fingers of his left hand along the top of the desk and opening a drawer with his right, as if he owned the place.

He did not even look up as she came in, just oozed a few words: 'Trying it for size.'

'It's too big for you, Toby,' she said.

He looked up at last and smiled. 'I thought you'd gone,' he said.

'Not only have I not gone, I'm not going.'

'That's not what he told me when he offered me the job.'

Her mind was full of questions. When had Bennet offered the job? How had Greene got back from Italy so quickly? It had been only a matter of hours. But she swallowed the questions. They were not important. Instead, she brushed past him with an 'excuse me' and sat in her chair. He sighed heavily as if all this were too boring for words. 'Come on, Paula, it's over. Go with good grace, like Clare when you . . .'

That did it. She screamed at him to get out and he backed away from her fury, bumping into Angela on the way in. The secretary waited until he was out of earshot, then said that Bennet was on the line.

'I'm not here,' she snapped. 'Get me my lawyer. And get me Frank Ormsby.'

If she had always thought of Lord Glenross as the father figure on the paper, then Frank Ormsby was the kindly uncle – stiff and distant sometimes, but, deep down, he had always been a friend. He could be counted on for advice, and now, when she wanted him again, he was on hand. He had suggested a little tea-shop off Gloucester Square, a quiet place where the waitresses wore white gloves, where china tea-cups tinkled and voices were never raised above a whisper.

Ormsby had listened without interrupting and when she had finished he said simply, 'He can't fire you.'

'Are you sure?'

'Of course he can't. Not from what you've told me. You have editorial control. He's trying to take it away from you. He can't do that. It's against the undertaking he gave the Government when he bought the paper. Five out of the seven national directors will be behind you.' He flapped his hand towards a plate. 'Have a tea-cake,' he said. 'They're delicious.'

She smiled and took one. Ormsby, she noticed, looked plumper. Over the past six months the tension had eased out of him. Semi-retirement obviously suited him. She looked around the room. It seemed like an oasis of relaxation in a desert of turmoil.

'This was a great idea,' she said.

Ormsby nodded. 'Alcohol intensifies a crisis. English tea puts it into perspective. I came here when Bennet threw me out. Ironically enough, I've just landed the first decent job since that day. I'm Chairman of the Computer Board. Just being set up.'

She toasted him in Earl Grey and he accepted her congratulations, then she asked, 'So, how do I play it?'

169

'Carry on as normal,' he said. 'If he has tried to appoint Greene, he's in serious trouble. I'll ask . . . no, I'll *tell* . . . him to attend an emergency meeting of the national directors. The story's out already.'

'Television has been on to me,' she said.

'Don't talk yet. Don't give him anything to complain about. Business as usual.'

She smiled and squeezed his hand, conscious of how lonely she had been over the past six months. 'You're terrific, Frank,' she said, and meant it.

He preened a little. 'I'm looking forward to it, believe me.'

'And what about the Stead story?'

He was cutting a square of tea-cake and she detected just a moment's hesitation. The knife stopped, then sliced gently through the cake. 'Ah,' he said. 'We're not on quite such firm ground there.'

'But that's what it's all about.'

'It's not,' he said and shook his head. 'It's about him firing . . .'

'It *is*,' she said, too loud. Heads turned. 'I'm going to publish that story.'

'You can't.' The voice was flat and unemotional. She blinked at him and he continued, his voice barely above a whisper. 'You're contravening the Official Secrets Act in receiving, let alone publishing, that document. The national directors couldn't support you in that.'

Paula felt a surge of impatience and it was an all too familiar feeling lately. 'An innocent man was murdered by the security services,' she said slowly and carefully. 'The Government is blatantly covering it up. They're using the Official Secrets Act purely to protect themselves.'

'That's not the point.'

'It *is* the point.'

'The point is, you're breaking the law. You're giving Bennet a stick to beat you with. I can't protect you if you do that. You must see that, Paula.' He paused and waited for a

170

reaction, but there was none. 'I want to see the story published just as much as you do.'

Paula was assaulted by a flash of *déjà vu*, of someone else saying the same thing.

'Do you, Frank?' she said.

'Of course I do. The story will get out. You're not the only white knight in Fleet Street. Give it to some scurrilous rag. That's the sensible thing to do.'

She shook her head. 'That's what Fleet Street's been doing for years. I thought I was different.'

'You are. You're responsible.'

'What's the use of responsibility if you can't tell the truth?'

He did not answer, looked away, avoiding her questioning gaze and made a fuss of selecting a cake. She watched him for a moment, then asked, 'What is the Computer Board?'

He shrugged and looked across the room. 'Oh, it's being set up to sort out the chaos in the industry – a sort-of quasi-quango.'

'Government funded?' she asked.

'Of course.' His gaze drifted round the room and settled on the tablecloth. 'Try one of these creamy things,' he said. 'Wonderful stuff.'

But her loneliness had returned and now it was even more acute. 'Oh Frank,' she said sadly. 'Have they got at you too?'

Throughout the late afternoon and early evening she had wandered listlessly and aimlessly around the West End. Once, she stood, in a half-dream, thinking of all that had happened, her memory snatching at images at random – a car crashing in Beirut, Ian touching her in the dark of the hotel room, Bennet in her bed, and, even then, never out of control . . . She stood by a news-stand, the *Standards* displayed by her elbow – a headline pronouncing *Register Power Struggle* with a photograph of her going into the Home Secretary's reception – but she did not see it. People jostled her on their way home from shops and offices, but

171

she scarcely noticed them. Then things seemed to slow down. She was sitting on a bench in Hyde Park. The traffic on Park Lane had eased and people were leisurely strolling past her, enjoying the evening sun. She glanced at her watch. It was eight. She had been in a dream for three hours, and it was long enough. She had had enough of self-indulgent self-pity. It was time to do something, and, as she got to her feet, she realised that she knew exactly what to do . . .

Walter Schiff was working alone on the eighth floor when she walked in. He looked round and grunted at her: 'He's not here.'

'It's not him I want to see,' Paula said. He shrugged and turned back to his work. 'I know what happened between you and Bennet, Walter,' she continued. He turned and, for the first time, a flutter of surprise flickered across his face. 'Do you think he's forgiven you?'

'No, I don't,' he said. 'He's been far too pleasant.'

She smiled. 'Can I buy you a drink?'

Another flicker of surprise. 'Sure you can buy me a drink, Paula, but what do I have to pay for it?'

An hour later she was standing on the pavement waiting for Bennet: in Park Lane. She had decided not to go up to his flat – better to get him on his own, outside. It was always the best policy not to fight a war on your opponent's ground, and, besides, something about him scared her. He was a big man. After last night he might feel . . . what was the word – proprietorial. He might feel he had some sort of territorial rights to her. She waited for ten minutes, then saw him come out and head for the Rolls parked twenty yards away. She flung away her cigarette and ran after him. He saw her, ignored her and carried on heading for the car. She reached him and tugged at his sleeve.

'You'd better see me,' she said.

He stopped. 'I'm late,' he snapped.

'It won't take long.'

172

He nodded at the chauffeur to wait and they walked slowly north. 'I have another story,' Paula said. 'Would you like to read it?' She pulled two typewritten sheets from her inside pocket, handed them over and watched while he read. His face gave nothing away, but she knew what he was thinking. He was wondering why Schiff would have squealed. It was a good question, and Paula knew the answer. If Bennet was discredited, then little Walter Schiff would stand to gain. It wasn't just for the price of a drink that he had unburdened whatever stood in place of his soul.

Bennet had told her the little man did not know the meaning of the word loyalty. She had gambled on Schiff and won.

Bennet crumpled the papers and pocketed them. 'Who told you about Pacific Universal?' he asked. 'My shareholders?'

'You did,' she said.

'Not all those details.'

She smiled. 'Several papers would jump at the story. And me.' He strode off and she had to trot to keep up with him. 'It's not the story I want to print, though,' she said.

He stopped and looked down at her, head cocked like a curious dog. 'You've come a long way, Paula,' he said.

'I've had good tuition.'

He looked at the sky for a moment, then back down at her. 'Give me a week,' he said.

'Why?'

'To get the *Mercury* contract through. There's an outside chance . . . nobody else is going to break the story. One week, and you can print what you damn well like.' And he was gone, without bothering to wait for an answer.

# Eighteen

It was her twenty-fourth paper and it wasn't one of the best. She stood in the newsroom reading the first edition, flipping through it, weighing it up: there were two good features and a brilliant piece from the American bureau on the new Republican hero. Sport looked bright. The leader was sharp and controversial and the news coverage, in general, did not lose out to the competition. The problem was the front page, splashing on a *Register*-commissioned poll count, showing that the Government had inched ahead of the other parties despite the latest Irish crisis. But it was a *so what?* main story – manufactured news – not what she or anyone else thought journalism was about.

Nor did David Stone seem pleased as he marched towards her, the paper in his fist. He reached her and threw it on the desk.

'It's like an election pamphlet,' he said.

This was no way for a young reporter to speak to his Editor. The only mitigating factor was that he was right.

'We'll make up for it next week,' she said, and smiled at him, then immediately realised that she had misread his mood. It wasn't the paper that was annoying him. He was pale and nervous. A boring edition didn't do that to people like David Stone.

'The Stead document's gone,' he said.

Questions leapt into her mind. Where? Who took it? Greene? Fowler? Who had it now? If it was the MoD, then whoever sent it to them was in trouble. All these questions surfaced in the two seconds it took her to reply.

'We've still got copies?'

'Yes.'

She looked across at the back bench, at Bennet and Greene chatting together, like conspirators.

'How long's it been gone?'

Stone shrugged. He didn't know.

'Ring the Ministry of Defence,' she said quickly. 'Alan will have the name of the duty officer.' And he was off. She didn't need to brief him. He knew what she was thinking. He knew the problems if there was an arrest in the air.

She went fast towards her office, smiling hellos at people, trying not to let her feelings show, aware that her paranoia was bubbling, aware that Bennet had planted a harvest of suspicion in her mind over the past six months. She did not want to show the signs of strain, in case anyone noticed and mentioned it to one of Bennet's people. She had to be all sweetness and light.

She had hardly time to gulp a mouthful of coffee when Stone knocked and pushed his way into her office. He was shrugging his shoulders and she knew what had happened – the old Whitehall stone wall again.

'Nothing,' he said.

'I'll bet.'

'What?' He looked puzzled, about to ask what she meant, when she started cursing, making a quick lap of the room, kicking out at the wastepaper basket, then she snapped her fingers, snatched the phone, tapped out a number and waited, biting her lip, praying for the woman to be in. Then someone answered.

'Mrs Stead? Paula Croxley.'

Stone watched as she spoke, just a few disjointed grunts, listening hard, then nodding and slamming the phone down again. She looked up at him and he could almost smell the anger and the frustration.

175

'They've arrested Andrew Osbourne,' she said. 'He's to appear in court on Monday morning.'

'That will make the whole story sub-judice.'

Paula nodded. 'And guess when the case comes up?'

It all fell into place for Stone. 'After the election,' he said. 'Christ. All that work.'

Paula began to laugh. 'Give me a week,' she said.

'What?'

She shook her head and glanced at her watch, then up at the door as Merton looked in.

'Has Bennet gone?' she asked.

'Yes. Just.'

'How's the second edition?'

'Proofing.'

'Right.' She snapped her fingers at Stone, then looked back at Merton. 'Set the Stead story,' she said, her eyes bright.

'Greene's here,' Merton said.

Stone made a tippling motion with his right hand. 'He'll be having a quick one,' he said.

'They won't print it,' Merton said solemnly.

'They'll do what I tell them,' said Paula.

'They won't.'

Paula ignored him and turned towards Stone again. 'Go on. Give the copy to Archie. Tell him I'll buy him a bottle of Pils. Two Pils.'

Stone made for the door as Merton continued shaking his head. 'Toby will be back for the edition . . .'

'Go to the pub,' she said to him. 'Keep him talking. Please, Alan.' Then she ran to the door and shouted after Stone. 'David. I don't want it read. No proofs. I don't care if it's full of literals. I'll look at it on the table.'

Then Merton brushed past her and smiled. 'I don't know if I'm being loyal or committing treason,' he said.

She squeezed his hand. 'Thanks, Alan,' she said, then she was off and running, the adrenalin pumping once again. This was Beirut again, this was another fight against a deadline.

She'd been through all this before, but always at the other end of the production line, never as the Editor, and never with such a story . . .

Old Archie was of the old school. He considered himself to be a craftsman. He had guided scores of young sub-editors through the complicated business of setting a page at speed. He knew what to do instinctively. He could cut a story and fit it like the most complex of jig-saws. He had seen generations of young sub-editors, anxious, biting their nails, checking their watches. Often he compared himself to an old sailor advising young officers. It was their job to make the decisions. It was his only to do what they asked, but he'd been at it for years and he knew before they did, and most of them had accepted his advice. Over the years he had learnt that the bumptious ones were the ones who disregarded his advice and the sad thing was that it was often the bumptious ones that made it up the ladder . . .

But the editor in front of him was not like that. He had always liked Paula, even when she was a young reporter and said 'fuck' a lot to prove she was tough. Now she was anxious and he could see why. He made up the page carefully, flipping lines of lead into place. Then it was ready. She looked at it and nodded and then did something no editor had ever done to him before. She kissed him on the cheek.

In the Feathers, Merton had insisted on another one. It was Greene's round. He couldn't back out. He would get himself a reputation. Besides, the man had seen the first edition. If anything happened, the phone in the corner would ring. The trouble was that Greene was getting bored and restless. Old Colin was telling some tale about Tehran when the Shah fell. It was a good story, even on the third telling, but now it was getting stale. Greene bought his drink and gulped it, checked his watch and said he was going upstairs, and Merton had no choice but to follow him.

Upstairs the desks were littered with copies of the first edition and with old proofs. Greene strode in, picked up the phone, grunted into it, then put it down.

'Nothing's been through the readers for the front,' he said.

'Hasn't it?' said Merton. 'Probably no change.'

'Paula would change the weather forecast.'

Merton shrugged, and something in his gesture made Greene look uneasy, then he was off and running for the stairs.

In the machine-room the job of plating-up had taken forever. To Paula it seemed as if the printers were on valium and her watch on benzedrine. A young printer yawned in her face – some kind of adolescent challenge to her authority perhaps – and she merely smiled at him. Then, finally, it was done and Ted Lamb was at her side with a copy of the front page. She snatched it from him greedily and this time her smile was genuine. 'It's fine,' she said.

The old rotary clattered above them and Lamb called out to someone to give it a bit more throttle.

Then they turned. A familiar voice had speared through the clattering of machinery. Greene was running towards them, pink-cheeked and angry, yelling: 'I haven't okayed this.'

'I have,' said Paula.

Lamb looked from one to the other as Greene rushed up to them, grabbed the page from Lamb's hands, scanned it and went even more pink.

'Bennet . . .' he said.

'Sod Bennet,' said Paula. 'I'm the Editor of this paper.'

Behind her, the machine picked up speed. Greene crushed the page and threw it from him as if it were contaminated, waved his arms at the crowd of printers, then bellowed in Lamb's ear: 'They'll lose their bloody jobs!'

Paula ignored them, seeing Merton and Stone hurrying towards her. She took two paces towards them, then froze as a terrible, familiar, grinding noise battered her eardrums. She

178

turned and looked imploringly at Lamb, then up at the old machine which had wheezed to a stop.

'Bloody thing,' Lamb said. 'Second time tonight.'

And Greene was smiling. 'Ah well,' he said, 'once we get the *Mercury*, we get a new press.' He ambled across to a phone hung on the wall and picked it up, then turned as Paula yelled at him: 'And do you know where that new press will be?' A sudden silence, the men looking up and listening. 'Birmingham,' she said.

Greene started dialling. 'That's not true,' he said.

She turned to Lamb. 'The Government has been trying to stop this story,' she said and brandished the proof in front of him like a matador's cape. 'Are you going to stop it as well?'

Lamb and the men began to walk slowly towards her. She had their full attention.

She turned to them and looked at the faces – suspicious men who had heard everything before; years of threat and counter-threat and payments at the last minute to keep the presses rolling. They were cynics to a man, but they were listening.

'They've bought Bennet,' she said. 'The price is: he gets the *Mercury*.'

Silence, except for the shifting of feet.

'You might say that's a bloody scandal,' she continued, 'and I think you're right. Or you might say, "So bloody what?" '

A number of heads nodded in agreement.

'I'll tell you bloody what.'

Behind her Greene slammed down the phone, cursed and began dialling again.

'Once Bennet gets the *Mercury*,' she said, 'that's it. Birmingham. Another Wapping. Worse. A hundred miles up the MI. The old independence of the *Register* is going.' Then she shook her head and corrected herself. 'Has gone. Tomorrow he'll be doing to you what he's done to me.'

One or two grinned at this, but most were serious. She turned to Lamb. 'Do you think he's your best friend?' she asked. There was no reaction. She glanced at the motionless

179

old machine, then back at him. 'Can you run it?' she asked softly. 'Can you run my last edition?'

Lamb said nothing, turned away and motioned a few of the men together. They went into a huddle. Paula closed her eyes and waited. When she opened them, Lamb was back in front of her and looking up at the Goss.

'I think I've an idea what's wrong with it, Miss Croxley,' he said.

In the Reform Club library, Bennet's mood was as mellow as the brandy in front of him. For a full two minutes Lord Bayswater had been sitting opposite him in silence, reading the *Register*, then he laid it on the coffee table and placed his glass on the headline: *Poll Shock As Election Nears: Government Moves Ahead.*

'A perceptive view of the political situation,' he said and poured himself more brandy. 'You should be a member here, Bennet. Glenross was.'

'I don't know anyone who would propose me.'

'You know me,' Bayswater said. 'Shall we go in for supper?'

It was a pleasant hour for both men. The claret was excellent, the beef tender. Bennet was pouring wine and paid no attention to the men at the next table who had just come in. He was in the middle of a story and barely noticed Bayswater leaning across and asking one of them if he could borrow his paper.

Bennet looked up and saw the old man looking at the *Register*. On the back Bennet could see Charlie Nicholas scoring for Arsenal which meant it was the London edition.

'There might have been one or two changes,' he said, 'if that's the last edition.'

Bayswater lowered the paper. He was chewing his lip. Then he abruptly got to his feet, dropped the paper on the table and murmured, 'I must get to a phone.'

Bennet watched him go, then flipped the paper over. The

new headline assaulted his senses: *Security Shock As Election Nears: Government Cover-up On M15 Killing.*

He got to his feet fast – too fast. Wine spilled. Then he did something that no one had ever done in the Reform Club library. He ran.

# Nineteen

It had taken her an hour to clear out her desk and write the three letters. She got to her feet, paced the room and looked out. It was a grey morning. Nothing moved. It was still too early for the bells of St Bride's to peal for worshippers. Through her open door she could see the newsroom, empty and cluttered from the night before. It would be another hour before the cleaners arrived and it seemed to Paula that she might be the only person awake in the city. Husbands would be with their wives, lovers with lovers, parents with their children. A pang of loneliness brought tears to her eyes. Angrily she rubbed them away with the back of her hand, went back to her desk, signed the letters, slipped them into envelopes and wrote a name on each: Alan Merton, David Stone, John Bennet.

Slowly she wandered out into the newsroom. She left Stone's letter on his desk, Merton's on the News Desk, then put the third in her pocket and sat at her old desk, the one they'd given her when she came back, all those years ago, no longer a secretary, but a fully-fledged reporter.

A noise made her look up. Bennet stood by the swing doors. He looked elegant in a leather jacket and slacks. The sweater would be cashmere, she thought – probably cost a hundred or more. He had a copy of the paper in his left hand and, as he approached, he whacked it against desks. Nothing about him surprised her now, not even the friendly smile.

He stopped a couple of paces from her and she could smell aftershave.

'I told you that you were an editor,' he said. 'I was wrong. You are a great editor.'

He tossed the paper on to the desk beside her. 'Terrific story,' he said. 'Magic. Dynamite. If I wasn't afraid you'd bite, I'd kiss you.'

She turned away from him and began to tremble and he did not know whether she was crying or laughing at him. He asked what was wrong and she turned. She'd been laughing at the absurdity of what he had said.

'What's wrong?' she mimicked, and got to her feet. 'Yesterday I had no judgment. I was stupid, naïve, unrealistic. I've wrecked the business, lost you the *Mercury* . . .'

He held one hand up for silence and with the other pulled a miniature tape recorder from his pocket, set it on the desk and pressed the *play* button. A voice she recognised from the Home Secretary's reception leaked into the room.

'It was a warning,' Lord Bayswater said. 'Not a police raid. That would have been counter-productive.'

She frowned, then blinked as Bennet's voice answered, 'Have you found the man who leaked it?'

'We know who he is,' Bayswater replied.

'Then why don't you arrest him? Make it sub-judice.'

'Because he won't admit anything, and we've no proof unless we get hold of the photocopy of that document.'

'It's going to come out.'

'Of course it is,' Bayswater said. 'It should. I'm not covering anything up. But I want to determine when and how.'

'After, not before, the election.'

'I know I can depend on you.'

Bennet leant across her, hit the *fast-forward* button for a moment, then tapped the *play* button again. Bayswater sounded angry now. 'Look, Bennet. There's no point in me talking to you in delicate shades of grey. The whole thing has got far too serious for that. I'm not talking about your interest or my interest. I'm talking about the national interest. And that is absolutely paramount. You know this country well

183

enough by now. If you serve it, it will serve you. I have no more to say. Thank you for coming . . .'

Bennet clicked the machine off. 'You see I haven't lost the *Mercury*, not yet. Bayswater thought I was a gentleman.' He pocketed the tape recorder and patted his pocket. 'I don't think they could stand another disclosure, do you? You've made it more difficult, that's all.'

Paula nodded. 'Did you have a tape recorder under the bed too?'

He shrugged. 'I had to save the paper.'

'You were saving yourself.'

'Do you think I enjoyed doing that?'

She looked at him. He had betrayed her in the worst possible way – did he enjoy doing it? 'Yes,' she said, 'in a way I think you did.'

His smile vanished. 'I did not,' he said violently, and took two steps towards her. Then he stopped, shook his head and apologised.

She picked up the envelope with his name on it and handed it to him.

'I can't go on here,' she said.

'I think you're right,' he said, putting it, unopened, into his pocket. 'I'll appoint Greene.'

She moved past him, heading back towards her office, then stopped as he called her name. He came up to her and turned her to face him.

'Are we thinking the same thoughts?' he asked.

She said nothing, waiting for him. 'How would you like to be Editor of the *Mercury*?' he asked.

She leant against the wall and closed her eyes as he continued. 'You're right. You've outgrown a weekly. You'd thrive on daily pressure.' She opened her eyes, looked up into his face. He seemed to be glowing with enthusiasm. 'Of course I'm flying a kite. I don't own the paper. But I didn't own the *Register*. Remember?'

She turned away from him, took her jacket from the peg on the back of her door and walked back through the newsroom towards the double doors and the stairs.

'Sleep on it,' he said. 'I'll give you a lift.'

'I have my car,' she said over her shoulder.

'*My* car,' he said.

She stopped and waited for him to catch up. 'Full colour tabloid,' he said. 'Two million print. We could slice off the bottom end of the *Mail*'s market . . .'

'With the same editorial independence,' she said, pushing open the doors.

'Sure,' he said, a pace behind. 'You still think that comes free? You dig out great stories . . .'

'Which you try to kill.'

'But without me, you've nothing to put them in.'

She stopped on the landing. 'I couldn't do it,' she said.

'With what you've learnt?'

He didn't believe that she couldn't do it and he was betting that she didn't believe it either . . .

The boys are back together again!

# AUF WIEDERSEHEN Pet.
## TWO

## by Fred Taylor

Now available: the second novel based on the hugely popular
series by Dick Clement and Ian La Frenais, probably the best
script-writing team in Britain today.

In response to an SOS from Barry, our heroes reassemble –
more than two years since their fond farewell on a building-
site in Germany.

This time the scene is Spain's notorious Costa del Crime and
Dennis, Neville, Oz, Barry, Wayne, Moxy and Bomber, still
chronically short of cash and hungry for travel, adventure and
mayhem, rebound from crisis to hilarious crisis.

They and their long-suffering wives and sweethearts find
themselves involved in scrapes that make the old days in
Dusseldorf seem like a dream cruise on the Rhine . . .

**HUMOUR/TV TIE-IN   0 7221 36749   £2.75**

# A selection of bestsellers from SPHERE

## FICTION

| | | | |
|---|---|---|---|
| STREET SONG | Emma Blair | £3.50 | ☐ |
| GOLDEN TRIPLE TIME | Zoe Garrison | £2.95 | ☐ |
| BEACHES | Iris Rainer Dart | £2.95 | ☐ |
| RAINBOW SOLDIERS | Walter Winward | £3.50 | ☐ |
| FAMILY ALBUM | Danielle Steel | £2.95 | ☐ |

## FILM AND TV TIE-IN

| | | | |
|---|---|---|---|
| MONA LISA | John Luther Novak | £2.50 | ☐ |
| BLOCKBUSTERS GOLD RUN | | £1.95 | ☐ |
| 9½ WEEKS | Elizabeth McNeil | £1.95 | ☐ |
| BOON | Anthony Masters | £2.50 | ☐ |
| AUF WIEDERSEHEN PET 2 | Fred Taylor | £2.75 | ☐ |

## NON-FICTION

| | | | |
|---|---|---|---|
| BURTON: THE MAN BEHIND THE MYTH | Penny Junor | £2.95 | ☐ |
| THE DISAPPEARED | John Simpson & Jana Bennett | £4.95 | ☐ |
| THE LAST NAZI: THE LIFE AND TIMES OF JOSEPH MENGELE | Gerald Astor | £3.50 | ☐ |
| THE FALL OF SAIGON | David Butler | £3.95 | ☐ |
| LET'S FACE IT | Christine Piff | £2.50 | ☐ |

*All Sphere books are available at your local bookshop or newsagent, or can be ordered direct from the publisher. Just tick the titles you want and fill in the form below.*

Name _____

Address _____

_____

Write to Sphere Books, Cash Sales Department, P.O. Box 11, Falmouth, Cornwall TR10 9EN.

Please enclose a cheque or postal order to the value of the cover price plus:

UK: 55p for the first book, 22p for the second book and 14p for each additional book ordered to a maximum charge of £1.75.

OVERSEAS: £1.00 for the first book plus 25p per copy for each additional book.

BFPO & EIRE: 55p for the first book, 22p for the second book plus 14p per copy for the next 7 books, thereafter 8p per book.

*Sphere Books reserve the right to show new retail prices on covers which may differ from those previously advertised in the text or elsewhere, and to increase postal rates in accordance with the PO.*